I0726860

LOW PLACES IN THE ROAD

Mark Stirling

WORKBOOK PRESS LLC
187 E Warm Springs Rd,
Suite B285, Las Vegas, NV 89119, USA

Website: https://workbookpress.com/
Hotline: 1-888-818-4856
Email: admin@workbookpress.com

Ordering Information:
Quantity sales. Special discounts are available on quantity purchases by corporations, associations, and others.
For details, contact the publisher at the address above.

Library of Congress Control Number:
ISBN-13:   978-1-952754-82-1 (Paperback Version)
                978-1-952754-84-5 (Digital Version)

REV. DATE: 10/17/2022

Low Places in the Road

By Mark Stirling

Trackers

It was a high, bright sky that day, perfect for fishin', dead wrong for school, but that's where we were headed. Me, Skinny Vinny and Piggyback Kidd, just walkin' along, mindin' our own business when along comes three Trackers on their bikes.

We didn't make up the name Trackers. That goes way back to my Granddaddy's day and describes anyone living along the railroad tracks that mark the edge of our side of town. We've all tried to make friends with the kids from over there. They just hate us. And it's not just me and Vinny and Piggyback. Any kid that's not like them, they just can't stand.

They came barreling over the railroad ninety to nothin' straight at Skinny Vinny. All I could think was *oh man, there's gonna be a fight*. They all hit the brakes and slid sideways, slinging rocks at both his bony legs. He cried out and stumbled backwards into Piggyback, then ducked behind the big guy.

Piggyback got his name because, when we were seven years old, he could carry four of us at a time on his back practically all the way across the playground. His real name is George Hermann Kidd. He's as fat as an old sow, but he's strong as a bull.

Herschel Garrett skidded to a stop a few yards away from us and hollered, "You girls late for Sunday School? Hidin' behind Blimp Butt ain't gonna protect you buncha sissies if we decide to teach you a lesson."

Vinny's pant legs were torn, and both his knees were bleeding. He was bunged up pretty good and wincing with pain. That worried me. Vinny Deluchi was hard to hurt. He hobbled out from behind Piggyback and said, "Who's hidin'?"

"Who's hidin'?" Herschel laughed. He was the biggest kid in James Bowie Junior High School, mainly because he had failed twice and was two years older than all of us. He absently touched the gold chain he always wore and said, "Looks to me like you are."

That chain must have been his most prized possession. Everyone knew his mother had given it to him when he was a little kid, just before she passed from cancer. She said it was because he was her little champion. I guess it's true that love is blind, because the last thing I thought of when I looked at Herschel was champion.

Nobody said a word until Piggyback dug his heels into the gravel road and said, "Herschel, we don't go looking for fights, but I'm gonna just lay it out real simple for you." He reached down and picked out a good-sized rock from the ground. Then he straightened up and he sighed kind of loud.

Now I was getting worried. Piggyback could be kind of a hypochondriac, but when he got riled up, he was a beast. Either way he was a great front man, mainly because he was like a giant shield.

"I see two options here, he said. "But before we talk about that, I should remind you that I can throw a baseball seventy-five miles an hour. Pretty accurately." Piggyback tossed the rock up and down in his hand as he talked. He was a catcher, not a pitcher, with the speed and power of a rocket launcher but the nuance of a bull on steroids. "My Dad says that a wink's as good as a nod to a blind mule, so try to concentrate on what I'm saying and consider this fair warning. Now, you can choose to let us by, or you can try to hurt my friends and take the chance of having this rock become the best-looking part of your face."

Then he pointed straight toward the stop sign that was about twenty yards behind the Trackers. He drew his arm back and hurled the rock. Flying fast as lightening and God's mind, the boom it made when it hit the sign sounded like a car backfiring. A big chunk of red flew off the middle of the sign, leaving a dent and a deep silver slash behind. It was a perfect shot.

Herschel's face twitched. I was waiting for steam to come out of his ears. The Trackers all looked at each other like they weren't sure what to do.

You could almost see them thinking it through. They wanted no part of a rock from this big 'ol catcher, but they hated to bail on a perfectly good opportunity to harass us. Then Herschel jerked his head, and his posse peeled out, pedaling for all they were worth, stirring up a cloud of dust so thick it made us cough. Herschel was the last to go. He circled in close, then suddenly leaned down and dropped me with a punch to the gut that felt like I'd been kicked by a horse. While I crawled on all fours, retching, Vinny strained to hold the big guy back. Herschel pedaled off and yelled back over his shoulder, "This is far from over, Rejects! We'll be back!"

Vinny let go of Piggyback's shirt and hobbled a few steps toward the Trackers' disappearing backs. "Where yhoose guys goin, huh?" he yelled back with his Brooklyn accent. "Y'aint so tough now!"

He threw an obligatory rock in their direction, just because he could. But all that was left of them was red dust hanging in the air.

As I climbed to my feet and dusted myself off, I looked over at the big guy and said, "Piggyback, you're a crazy hero today."

Piggyback looked to the sky and grinned. "How

long have those guys been dogging us, Hats? Seems like we've always gotten the short end of the stick." He threw his fist into the air and shouted, "Not today, baby!"

None of us said what we all knew—that it would be a short victory. Herschel and his crew would find a way to make us pay.

History Class

We finally limped into the building, arms around each other, looking like we had come back from a war. Piggyback and I were practically dragging Vinny, who was in between us. We were all covered in road dust head to toe. Fortunately, we were late and there were only a couple of people in the hall.

We headed straight for the restroom to clean up a little before dropping Vinny off at the nurse's office. Without offering some giant explanation, we just told the nurse that Vinny fell off his bike and we hurried to History.

When Piggyback and I got to History and looked through the skinny glass window on the door, we panicked a little.

Mr. Rite was in our room with some pointy-nosed lady we didn't recognize.

He looked proud as a peacock in his brown corduroy

jacket, vintage 1978. The lady was standing beside him, dodging his flailing hands, which were a signature part of every one of his presentations. Mr. Rite was famous for saying very little, yet sucking all the oxygen out of the room while doing it. For a principal, he was the most nervous speaker ever. Every assembly, he dropped the papers he used to speak from. Every single time.

But we were in for it, for sure. What a day to be late.

Piggyback was still feeling it from earlier and decided to take charge. "I'm just gonna be honest and let the chips fall. C'mon, Hats!"

Of course, he didn't quietly enter the class and take a seat. Not the Kidd. He took a step back and busted in, saying, "We're so sorry that we're late, Mr. Rite and whoever this nice lady might be. But we were unavoidably detained against our will. Pretty sure that's illegal. Our friend Vinny Deluchi is in the nurse's office right now because he was injured by Herschel Garrett and his future cellmates. I doubt you'll even see Herschel at all today. He usually skips after he commits a crime."

Mr. Rite looked at us over the rims of his glasses. "All right, Mr. Kidd, that'll be enough. I'll speak with you and Mr. McCleary about this matter after class. You boys find a seat, please. Now, where was I? I'll recap and get on with it. After a long search for the right fit for a History teacher to replace someone of Mrs. Angelo's caliber, I am very happy to report that we have found an outstanding teacher for the job."

The whole time Mr. Rite was yammering on, this new lady was shuffling her feet back and forth and looking up and down like she had to pee.

Mr. Rite went on. "Please allow me to introduce your new teacher and our newest staff member, Ms. Carol Meadows. Ms. Meadows, here are today's rolls and I will look in on you throughout the day. Class, please give Ms. Meadows your undivided attention and best behavior. Have a great first day."

The pointy-nosed woman watched him leave, then turned to the rest of us. "All right class, as Mr. Rite said, I am Ms. Meadows." She wrote her name on the whiteboard like we were in second grade.

Puleease!

"Before we get started, young man who just came in, would you please remove your hat? We're indoors and its good manners to take it off."

All I could get out of my mouth was "But. . ."

"No buts, please."

I looked around the room. A couple of Herschel's friends were smirking. Piggyback's jaw was set, and my best friend, Claire, looked like she was watching a car wreck in slow motion.

The pointy-nosed woman frowned. She looked at her seating chart. "Young man. Finn McCleary. Your hat."

Slowly, I slid my hat off. I could feel my hair spring free in a million directions. I didn't need a mirror to know what it looked like—a bright orange mop. It flopped over my forehead in front, stood up all around, and curled down the back of my neck, covering most of a birthmark shaped like a map of Idaho. Before she left, my mom used to call me the Idaho Kid and give it an extra kiss at night before bed. It seemed special to me then. But now it was just big and red and ugly, and I hated it.

I heard the snickers echo across the room, and my face grew hot.

"Thank you, Finn," Ms. Meadows said coolly. She gave the class a stern look, and the laughter died. "I must tell you all that I am new to your region. However, I did move here a couple of months ago, to acclimate myself to the weather and begin to study your curriculum. You see, I come from the Northeast." She scanned the room with a nervous smile. "Now, I know you've been without a steady instructor for some time. However, I plan to close that gap quickly and get back on track immediately, working steadily in concert with each of you."

I glanced around and saw a few kids still smirking behind their hands. Claire looked like she wanted to bean someone with one of her crutches. My cheeks still burning, I leaned over toward Piggyback's desk and whispered, "What the heck is wrong with her index finger? Every time her voice goes up, her finger points up. I think she's reaching for her umbrella. She's freakin' Mary Poppins, dude!"

Piggyback snickered. "Holy crap, Hats. She does do that. So weird."

She called roll and we hooted and hollered a little bit like we always do during roll call. Ms. Meadows had to get on to Frieda Parks. She had her book propped up on the desk in front of her and her phone in the book and she was steadily texting. Ms. Meadows glanced at her handy seating chart again. "Miss Parks! Do you really think I can't see that phone? Put it up, now."

Frieda just glared from under her bushy eyebrows and the stringy bangs hanging in her face. Hermann chimed in with his usual level of intelligence. "She didn't do nothin', lady!"

We couldn't wait for the bell to ring us out of captivity, but as we were pouring out the door, Ms. Meadows called me back. Piggyback, helping Claire with her crutches, looked over and frowned.

I gave him a thumbs up. *"It's cool."*

When the rest of the class had gone, Ms. Meadows gave me an apologetic smile. "You must be pretty angry with me right now."

"You didn't know," I said. I was trying to be fair, even though I was still a little mad. "But Mrs. Angelo always let me wear my hat. All my teachers do."

Her smile got a little edge to it. "I'm not Mrs. Angelo. Nor am I 'all your teachers.'" Then she sighed. "You have a lovely head of hair, Finn. Like a poet. But that's beside the point. I was always taught that for a young man to wear a hat indoors was a sign of disrespect."

"I'm not being disrespectful," I said. "I'm just more comfortable wearing a hat."

"The school rules specify no hats inside the building." She reached into her desk drawer, pulled out a printed list of rules, stapled at one corner, and pointed.

"Nobody follows those," I said. "They're a hundred years old."

"Maybe so. But until Mr. Rite gives me something to replace them with, they're all I've got. And I don't see anybody else trying to wear a hat in class."

I didn't answer. I knew why my other teachers let me get away with wearing hats, and I didn't want to tell a perfect stranger it was because they felt sorry for me.

Finally, I said, "Nobody else has hair like mine. And don't tell me to just get it cut, because I tried that, it's no better."

"That's your choice, of course," she said. "I just wanted to say I was sorry for embarrassing you."

"Then I can wear my hat tomorrow?"

She tapped the list of rules. "Not as long as these say otherwise. But I should have spoken to you about it in private."

Public. Private. What difference did it make? This pointy-nosed newbie was ruining my life.

"Sure. Right. Thanks for nothing," I said, and stomped out of the room.

Piggyback was waiting for me outside. "Ooooh, Finn," he said, in a high-pitched voice. I jammed my cap onto my head and shot him a dirty look. It shut him up, but it didn't keep him from snickering when he thought I wasn't looking.

All I could do was hope for an alien invasion before tomorrow morning. Surely space aliens would have some kind of ray gun that would change Ms. Meadows' mind and wipe my classmates' memories of my flaming orange mophead.

The Verdict

Claire was waiting for us in the stairwell, and the three of us gathered for a quick review.

Piggyback slung his arm around me, ducked his head into our little triangle, and said, "Okay, I say we put it out of its misery before it's too late. She's gonna be more trouble than a box of puppies."

Claire shifted forward over her crutches and said, "Piggyback, you're crazy. I think she was just nervous on her first day."

I stared at Claire. "Good grief, Sweet Face, you like everybody! I can't even wear my hat. I'm quitting school!"

Claire rolled her eyes and stamped one crutch on the ground. "Hats, don't be an idiot. Nobody cares about your hair but you. No one who matters, anyway." This girl, this unbridled, fearless friend of mine, was born with a rare genetic bone disease that affected her hips and legs. She had progressively gotten weaker in those areas each year since she had moved to town when we were eight. But she was battle tested, and boy did she hate to lose.

She stared at me with fierce brown eyes until finally, I mumbled, "Okay, okay. We're stuck with her. Maybe we can break her in."

I wasn't sure how I felt about Ms. Meadows. She'd apologized, sort of, but she hadn't changed her mind about my hat. She seemed strict, but she wanted to be fair. Maybe she'd come around. After all, she knew nothing about nothing in the south. It was up to us to educate her.

"She might turn out to be okay," I said, and Piggyback's mouth dropped open.

Before he could say anything, Skinny Vinny finally showed up. "Well, I'm alive, Compadres! I had to go home and get different pants. Had to eighty-six the other pair. That's why it took so long."

I grabbed Vinny by the arm and said, "You could have texted one of us, Vin. We didn't know what happened to ya."

Piggyback began to examine Vinny up and down like he was a doctor or something. And he started asking all kinds of questions: Are you feeling dizzy? Are you still in pain? Blah, blah, blah. Vinny this, Vinny that. It was kind of weird for a minute, to be honest.

Vinny waved him away. "I'm okay, Piggyback. For crying out loud, you were there. It was no big deal."

Everything was "no big deal" to Skinny Vinny. He'd seen some tough breaks for a kid our age. He came to our town from Brooklyn, New York, with his Uncle Gino after both his parents were killed in a robbery at their fish market. Vinny was only six years old when that happened. Nothing scared Vinny for long, not even a bunch of Trackers led by a demented bully who'd rob his own brother without hesitation.

Thank God, we had to get to class, which put a stop to the medical interrogation. Piggyback was a real mess with one of his shoelaces untied. He was practically breaking his neck tripping down the hall. When he reached down to tie his shoe, his iPad bounced out of his backpack and landed right in front of Mr. Jenkins, our science teacher.

"Get that thing in your backpack, Mr. Kidd. I don't wanna see it again."

"Aye, aye, Sir," Piggyback replied, with a mock salute. He finally managed to catch up with me, all out of breath.

"Hats," he bellowed, as he gasped for air. "You cannot like this teacher, man?"

I shrugged and said, "I'm not happy with her. I'm just not rushing to judgment. Maybe we can mold her, or at least persuade her, you know?"

He didn't look convinced. I wasn't either, but I patted Biggun' on the back anyway and said "We're gonna be late. Stop worrying so much, will ya? If you get an ulcer in that gut, we'll have to hire a search party, not a doctor."

Piggyback rolled his eyes. "Very funny, Mophead. Next time, remind me to laugh."

Dad

My Dad was an architect before he served in the military. Sometimes he worked from home, sometimes from his office, but I never knew for sure if he'd be there when I got home from school.

I was relieved to hear the screech of his table saw when I got home. If he was in his workshop, I wouldn't have to pretend to be in a good mood. He hadn't paid too much attention to anything since my little sister died and my mom left. Don't get me wrong. He's a great dad. He fixes me breakfast and watches old movies with me. And makes sure I get to school and tries to teach me right from wrong.

"Jesus, Mary and Joseph!" he'll say when I do something stupid. Then he'll have a "Dad talk" with me. Those are more like lectures, but he tries. And it's not like I don't know how he feels. I do. But my feelings, I struggle with. Ever since Mom left, my Dad had kept her telephone number pinned under a magnet on the fridge. Some days I wanted to rip it off and burn it. Other days, I came within an inch of calling her. I do my best to contain my weird feelings and try to handle all my school stuff without concerning my Dad. He has a full enough plate without me adding to things.

I was glad it was movie night. I not only looked forward to watching, but there was little conversation that was necessary. It was easy to transport yourself into a good movie with great characters. Humphrey Bogart is one of my Dad's favorites had become one of mine. I think we've probably seen everything he made. He always played someone who was tough, no-nonsense, but smart.

The sound from the shop came to a sudden stop. I went to the back door to see if Dad was headed in for the evening. At first, I didn't see him at all. Then he came running out of his shop holding a rag over his left hand. I hadn't seen my Dad run in years. I quickly opened the door and he was there in a flash.

"What the heck happened, Dad?"

"Get the first aid kit, Finn. I'm okay. I just cut my finger pretty good. Hurry up, boy." Blood was dripping on the kitchen floor as my Dad made his way to the sink. I got the kit from the hall closet and brought it straight to the sink. He had taken the rag off his hand and I thought I was gonna faint.

"Dad, we gotta get you to the hospital."

"Hand me that gauze and look away, Bubba." I didn't want to look, but I couldn't help myself. My Dad made a face but didn't make a single sound as he took the flesh that was hanging off his middle finger and pressed it back into place. I opened the bottle of peroxide and he poured it over his wound. It bubbled and fizzed like crazy.

He nodded toward the first aid kit and said, "Now, tear off a piece of that tape and put it around my finger. Not too tight." I did as he asked and felt a little nauseous for him.

He leaned on his right forearm for a second as he held the medicine cabinet door. Then he opened it and took out the aspirin bottle. He opened it with his teeth and swallowed a mouthful of tablets.

"So, tell me," he said, "what's the team looking like for next season, Son?" I knew he just wanted to take his mind off the pain. But we often discussed baseball, so I obliged.

"Well, pretty good, I think. I believe that we've talked Will Sagan into playing this season." He's a southpaw and can pitch or play second.

"No joke? That's just what we need this year."

"Yeah, I agree, Dad."

"That's good news, Finn," he said. "Why don't you get your shower now? You may have to help me out with dinner. It's movie night, you know? Let's get it rolling, okay?"

"Okay, Dad."

Who was this man? Rambo? I didn't bug him anymore about seeing a doctor because he acted like it was no big deal. But I sure wanted to.

I had heard all the war stories for years about he and his unit in Afghanistan, but you get to a point where you say, yeah, right. This is just my Dad. But now, replaying some of the things he had told me before, I realized they weren't just stories at all. Geez Louise, My Dad was way tougher than I ever gave him credit for.

I looked over at his bandaged hand and thought, no way was I complaining to him about not being able to wear my hat in class.

Mr. Red

We rode the tin can to school the next morning. Mr. Red, our driver, grinned when I climbed aboard. He was an old, kind of goofy guy with big ears and a lot of kids made fun of him. But he always said good morning like he was glad to see you. Just like always, we shot our "finger guns" at each other. He was quick on the draw for an old guy.

Once we were settled in our seats, we picked up Allen Wells. I noticed after Mr. Red closed the door behind Allen, he made a fist toward his chest, like people do when they need to burp. Then he reached in his shirt pocket and popped a large pill that looked like a Tums or a Rolaid. I'd never seen him do that before.

As usual, Allen boarded the bus staring at a paperback. He has worn thick glasses ever since I can remember. Probably from reading strain. Allen is the biggest bookworm I know. He always has a book in his hand, like he can't wait to find out what happens next in the story. I like him. I always have. But he is kind of a nerd.

As Allen made his way toward the back of the bus where he always sat, Nick Blanchard stuck his foot out in the aisle and tripped him. When he stumbled and dropped his book, Nick said, "Hey four-eyes, you need to watch where you're going."

Nick Blanchard was a pretty popular guy. He played football and the girls liked him, but he was a creep. I never had any run-ins with him probably because I played baseball and he thought I was in the athletic clique. To me, he was no better than the Garretts. No better at all. Mr. Red saw Allen fall in his mirror, he yelled back," Hey, hey, hey! What's going on back there?"

Allen Wells got up to his feet and said," I'm okay, Mr. Red. Just tripped." I picked Allen's glasses up from underneath one of the seats where they slid, and I handed them to him. He looked at me, trying to smile, and said, "Thanks Hats, can't believe they didn't break this time."

As we arrived at school, everyone began to bunch

up toward the front of the bus to get off. Just before we got to the steps, Mr. Red turned toward the back and said," Mr. Blanchard, I'll need you to meet me just outside the bus."

"I've got to go see Coach Barnes before class, man."

"Oh, we're going to see Coach Barnes, alright." After we all got off the bus, Mr. Red got down from the steps of his bus and said, "Come with me, boy. We're going to the field house and discuss your future."

I could hardly believe my eyes. Mr. Red was a good six inches shorter than Nick and not half as heavy. But as they veered from the sidewalk across the grass, angling toward the football field, Mr. Red was dragging that boy by the arm in a hurry. Kids on the sidewalks stopped to watch this escort. Nick was steadily telling him how he couldn't do that. But our little Mr. Red was sure doing it. He wasn't arguing with Nick at all. He just marched his rear in front of everybody, straight to see Coach Barnes. I wanted to clap so bad. I personally loved the fact that Mr. Red was bypassing Mr. Rite so he could hit this guy where it was bound to hurt. I found out later in the day that Coach Barnes, the football coach, had suspended Nick for two games. I bet he never underestimates the power of a bus driver again.

Research Assignments

We spent the next week in Mary Poppins' land of hypnosis. The Garretts and their cronies teased me about my mophead for a few days, and I caught some of the other kids laughing behind my back. I pretended not to care, even though I did. There was no alien invasion, but after a while, Jason Abernathy got a bad case of the hiccups during English class, and everybody pretty much forgot about my hair. Nothing much else happened, except that Mr. Red had a birthday and wore a weird hat for about three days. It was pretty funny, but he brought us all cupcakes, so nobody made fun of him—at least, not to his face.

On Monday, I was hoping to catch Claire alone before class, but I was out of luck. Everybody else arrived early too, I guess so we could mentally prepare each other. Piggyback came in yappin' with gossip. "Hey, did you guys hear about the girl fight over at Clark's grocery yesterday?"

Claire immediately stopped writing on her book cover and put her pen down. "No. What girl fight?"

"Yeah, Eugenia Rojas and Frieda Parks got into it pretty good in the parking lot. There was enough hair on the ground after that scrap to make a wig."

By the look on Claire's face, I thought she was going to grill Piggyback, but she just asked softly, "Do you know why they fought?"

Piggyback shrugged.

I didn't know much about it, but I told her what I'd heard. "Yesterday Freida posted on Facebook that Eugenia stole something from her. I didn't pay any attention to it. I mean, I wouldn't put it past her, but Frieda's lied before, so who knows?"

Hermann loudly cleared his throat from the back of the room and without lifting his head from the desk, said, "Nobody stole anything. Frieda was picking on Gene's little brother. I know, I was there."

Hermann would know. He was cousin to the Garrett bunch, but he usually stayed out of trouble. Now I was getting interested. Everybody knew that if you messed with a Garrett you faced all the Garretts. Same thing with the Rojas bunch.. Mess with one, every one of them came runnin'. So, it was my turn to ask Hermann a question. "So, Hermann, what did Frieda do to Billy?"

He half lifted his head. "Ask Gene. Ain't my place, Hats."

Eugenia probably just wanted an excuse to punch somebody. She was just that kind of girl. But I didn't say that, because I knew it would upset Hermann. Instead I said, "Here we go, guys. Mary Poppins, center stage."

For someone whose desk was so neatly arranged, Ms. Meadows was kind of a mess. She came to class every day with her hands full of books and folders. Then, instead of getting to her desk safely with the load of books first, she always started taking off her sweater before sitting the books down. She usually kind of avalanched the books all over the desk saying, "Nuts" or "Jiminy Christmas," like she'd just stepped out of an old movie.

Today it was just an extended "Welll! Good Morning, everyone. We're going to get right to it this morning. I have a new assignment for you and it's going to take some effort and cooperation. Each of you will be partnered with a classmate of my choosing and you will work together on a research assignment for which you each will receive a test grade."

Claire stood the silence as long as she could, then delicately stated, "Um, Ms. Meadows?"

"Yes Miss?"

"Mrs. Angelo had all our assignments outlined on a syllabus that we have followed all year long."

"Well, Miss Hanover, I've restructured the syllabus a bit." She gave us a smile. She looked prettier when she smiled. "Class, I am fully aware that having a new teacher is an adjustment. But having a new class is as well. Now, I know that not all of you are going to like the way I teach and to be perfectly frank with you, I'm not going to like the way all of you approach learning. But we are all people and we're in this together, so I will fight with and for you in that pursuit." Out of nowhere, the door flew open and Herschel Garrett busted into the classroom. Ms. Meadows looked his way and said, "There's a seat in the back, young man. You're awfully late. Do you have a note for me?"

Hershel didn't even look her way and mumbled, "For what?" She ignored his insolence and carried on.

There was something about this pointy-nosed teacher that struck a chord in me in that moment. The way she curled her lips under and the way she looked at Herschel, unintimidated. And I loved the fact that she didn't stand in one place all the time like Mrs. Angelo.

I must have been coming down with something because I suddenly found myself rooting for this outsider..

"And guys," she went on, "you must understand that my job is to teach you. So, what do you say I do the best I can to do my job and you can meet in the middle somewhere? Now, where was I?"

Claire raised her hand. "You were explaining research assignments."

"Thank you, Claire. Okay, I'm going to read off your names in pairs. Now, I think it may be beneficial to work in blocks of four. So, after you get a partner, partner again. This will help each pair see and hear interactive debate from the other. Please write down your partner's name. We'll get to subject matter next time. All right. George and Willard. Tommy and Marshall. Vinny and Rebecca. Claire and Eugenia."

Claire made a little squeak like she couldn't believe what she was hearing. Then Ms. Meadows dropped another bombshell. "Finn and Herschel."

Finn and Herschel? What? Wait. No! My head was exploding. What was she trying to do, kill me? I looked over at Claire and saw disbelief on her face as well. I knew this lady didn't realize what kind of crazy she was unleashing in her own classroom, but we sure did.

Herschel

Herschel started the fireworks from the back of the room. Standing up with one foot on his desk seat and his right thumb to his ear, his pinky pointing straight down, he made the sound of a ringing telephone. *Dddddring, ddddddring.* "Oh, Ms. Meadows, I have New Hampshire on the line. The lady says you left your brains in your old apartment and you're gonna need to claim it before the end of the day."

Nearly the whole class died laughing. Those who didn't wanted to climb inside our desks. I think Ms. Meadows was in shock. I knew one thing. I wasn't working with that jackass. No way.

I guess it was no surprise that Herschel had turned out to be so mean. He'd lost any good influence when his mother passed, and his dad, who everyone called Screwy Louie, never was much of a parent. When he wasn't on the job at the ironworks, he stayed too drunk to hit the ground with his hat. Many a time, he was found asleep in his deer blind surrounded by empty beer bottles. But after his wife died, he just lost all control over his kids. It made me appreciate my dad a lot more.

I might have even felt sorry for Herschel if he hadn't been such a jerk. And let's face it. If it were raining hundred dollar bills, Herschel would be out looking for a dime he lost some place.

Ms. Meadows took a moment to look around the room. She settled on Skinny Vinny. "Mr. Deluchi, will you come up here please?"

Vinny had his head on his desk when Ms. Meadows called him to the front, and when she called his name his head shot up like a dog that just heard a potato chip bag rattle. "Me?" he asked her sleepily.

"Yes, please, come here. Do me a favor, Vinny and hand these outlines out to everyone. And Vinny . . . no hurry doing it."

"Yes, Ma'am."

She turned toward Herschel. "Oh, Mister Garrett,

since it's obvious that you are starving for attention, I'd hate to be the one to deny you something you seem so in need of. I also want you to know that I appreciate extemporaneous speech. And to reward you, you've won a new home for the rest of the school year. Right here beside my desk at the front where everyone can enjoy your wit. Come, come, sit by me."

Man, ol' Herschel didn't care for that one bit. He was fuming.

He slapped the side of his desk away from his leg and began his walk of shame. Sauntering toward the front, he brushed back his greasy hair and pulled his chin up as far as he could, as if he didn't care.

He scowled down at his desk for the rest of the class, and when Ms. Meadows gave us our list of topics to choose from, he wadded his into a ball and lobbed it at the trash can. It hit the rim and bounced in. Two points.A few minutes before the end of class, Claire heaved herself up and headed toward the door. She always tried to beat the rest of the class to avoid traffic with her crutches, which meant that, despite her spaghetti legs, I was always chasing her.

The bell rang, and the rest of us filed out. As I passed Herschel's desk, he slid out of his seat and bumped me hard with his shoulder. "We're not partners, Freakazoid," he said, his eyes small and mean. "I'd drink bleach before I'd partner with a Reject like you."

"Promises, promises," I said, and ducked past him, losing myself in the stream of students before he could retaliate.

The Invitation

As usual, Piggyback was waiting for me. He cleared a path to where I was, the rush of bodies parting around him like water curves around a boulder. "Hey Pig," I said, "I'll meet you at your locker."

"Okay, see ya in a minute."

I circled back, keeping an eye out for Herschel, then went back to Ms. Meadows' room. She was straightening the papers on her desk, but looked up when I stepped into the room. Now that I was here, I felt a little foolish. "I, uh, I wanted to apologize for Hershel. We're not all like that."

She gave me a grateful smile, and for a moment, I thought she might cry. Then she straightened her shoulders and said, "Thank you, Finn. That's very kind of you."

I hurried out before she could say anything else, hoping to catch Claire before our next class started. I caught her just outside of Science class. "Hey Claire, wait up!"

She paused and looked back over her shoulder.

"Hats, don't you have to get your book from your locker?"

"Yeah, but I was wondering if you were gonna be busy Saturday morning, say around ten thirty?"

She readjusted her crutches. "Well, let's see, I have soccer practice, kung fu lessons and a yoga class. But other than that, no." She pulled back a finger each time she named one of these absurd activities, like she was counting them off. What a clown.

"Shut up, Claire." I thumped her gently in the arm. "You're like the funniest human being on the planet, seriously. Anyway. . ." I looked down at my feet, feeling suddenly awkward. "The Fair starts Saturday and I was wondering if you'd like to go with me?"

She looked down at the floor like she was thinking about it. Then she destroyed me with a sideways smile and said, "Call me after school and we'll talk about what time, okay?"

I hurried to class feeling strangely light. Piggyback came in late, and I realized I'd forgotten to stop by his locker. He looked at me funny all through class, but I didn't care. I didn't even care that Herschel was probably going to kill me. I couldn't stop grinning. It wasn't romantic feelings that I felt for Claire. She was my very best friend. I felt comfortable talking to her. She had a way to put me at ease. And I needed that. It had always been like that between the two of us.

The Fair

Dad had agreed to drop us off on Saturday morning. When we rolled up to Claire's place, she was standing on her front porch propped up on her crutches, with one elbow on her porch rail. She ambled over to the car, and Dad got out to help her in.

I sat in the back seat and let Claire sit in the front because there was more leg room. Dad surprised me by starting the conversation. My Dad's not what you would call a talker, especially not since Abigail died and Mom left, but Claire has this way of provoking people to talk without really meaning to. He said, "Claire, I haven't seen you in a while."

"Yes Sir," she said. "But I have seen you in the choir at church. Your singing is very good, Mr. McCleary."

Dad smiled, his cheeks turning a little pink. "Well. . . thank you. You know Finn sang in the choir until his voice started changing and he decided to stop participating. I told him it wouldn't last and that he owed it to his talent to keep it up. Have you heard him sing, Claire?"

"Hey Dad, you better slow down, the turn is right up here on the left."

Thankfully, my Dad eased up on the bragging as we arrived. "Yep, kids, here we are. Now listen, Finn, you have enough money, right?"

"Yes Sir."

"Okay, Claire, you good?"

"Yes Sir."

My Dad had to nail down every detail. I'm surprised he didn't frisk me. "I'll pick you up right here at seven o' clock, okay?"

We just wanted to go. Exasperated, I said, "Thanks, Dad."

"Yeah," Claire said. "Thank you, Mister Mac."

We were out of the car in a flash and moving through the parking lot to the front gate.

Claire hit me in the butt with her right crutch and we joined the crowd of fair goers.

After we made our way through the gauntlet of the main gate, the crowd dispersed into a thousand directions. We decided to take it straight up the runway and enjoy it all. We rode some rides, went in a bunch of exhibits and made each other laugh a hundred times. We dodged the Garretts a couple of times on the midway. And by lunch time we needed a break.

Claire got right behind me and put one crutch over my shoulder, using it to point the direction she wanted me to go. She led me over to a small lunch area that was set up like a sidewalk café, and we sat down at a tiny table for two. Claire said, "Isn't this quaint?"

I glanced around. "I'm not sure I've ever really experienced quaint before. But if you think it is, then okay, quaint it is."

"Well it is, and now you know, Mister." She grinned, but her face looked a little pale.

I put a hand on her arm to steady her. "Are you tired?"

"A little," she admitted, "but I'm okay."

After we ate hamburgers we just sat and talked for a long time. At first it was just small talk. Then the conversation turned. "Finn, can I ask you something very personal?"

"Of course, you can."

"How long has it been since you've seen your Mom?"

I had just told her she could ask. But that was out of left field. I wasn't ready for the fun to be over. So, I switched gears. "Hey they got Icees over there. You want an Icee? I'm thirsty, are you? I'll be right back. You still like black cherry, right?"

I was already moving and took as long as I could to get back with the Icees. But I knew it wouldn't deter Claire. If she could, she'd bandage the whole county. I made a last-ditch effort to change the subject. "You sure you don't want to talk about how hot Oliver thinks you are? Or how about how far your telescope can see? No, I guess you don't. Geez, Claire!"

She just stared through me.

I sighed. "It's complicated."

"You know you can tell me about it, Hats," she said gently. "It might help just to say it out loud."

"My family is screwed up, Claire. I don't even like thinking about it. Much less talking about it."

"All families are screwed up," she said. "Just tell me."

I took a deep breath and blew it out. "You know I had a sister, right? Abigail. Abby. It was before you moved here."

"I've heard people talk. She drowned?"

I nodded. "She was only three and a half. And it happened at my Aunt's house, my Mom's sister, in a kiddie pool. She drowned in a foot of water. My Mother left her there for the day and my Aunt turned her back for just a couple of minutes. My sister had an asthma attack and ended up face down in the water. It was a weird accident, but my Mother always felt it was her fault. Fact of the matter is, it wasn't my Mom's fault, it was mine. Before she took Abby to my Aunt's, she asked me if I could watch her. I had already planned to play baseball with some of the boys, but I just didn't feel like babysitting. If I had, she'd be alive today." I looked away, swallowing hard, but Claire was right. It did feel good to tell someone. When I got control of my voice, I went on. "My mother's guilt got her addicted to prescription medication and eventually a divorce from my Dad. Pretty picture, huh?"

She put a hand on my arm. "Bad things happen. I've read lots of books, Hats, and one thing I've learned is that sometimes things just aren't anybody's fault."

"Look, Claire, this is depressing. I thought we were having fun today."

Claire touched my face with the tips of her fingers and I knew she understood that I needed to stop talking about it for now.

She cleared her throat and looked at me and said, "You don't have to answer this now, but I want you to think about this: I think you and I should go on the bus to see your Mom one weekend."

I stood up. If she kept talking, I'd either cry or get mad, and I didn't want to do either in front of Claire. "Come on, Sweet Face, let's go see the fortune teller up there in the purple tent. Want to?"

She gave a sad little sigh and said, "Sure, Hats. That sounds great."

The Fortune Teller

We got to the tent that said *Have your fortune told*. Another sign read *One customer at a time*. I let Claire go in first. It took her a good ten minutes to come out, and when she did, she looked both dazed and angry.

"Well? I asked. "Was it creepy?"

She shrugged. "It was a little weird. Go on and try it."

I walked in and there sat this old gray-headed woman, her elbows propped on a table and her fingers laced together forming a cup for her long, wicked looking chin to rest in. And she said, "Please have a rest in my chair, boy." The small table between us had some velvet drapery over it and a bunch of little ivory-looking trinkets spread all over it.

She asked if I'd ever had my fortune read before and I said no I never had. And then she looked me straight in the eyes and leaned in close to the table. Her eyes were white. High cloud white. Now she had my attention for sure.

In a raspy voice, she said, "Whatcha doin' in here if you don't believe in fortune tellin'?"

I don't know how she knew that, but let me tell you, she scared the mess out of me. I scooted my chair back a couple of inches and said, "Um, I didn't say I don't believe. I just never tried it before."

"If you wanna do this, put your dollar on the table."

I dug in my front pocket for a crumpled-up dollar that I'd gotten back from the Icee guy and put it cautiously on her table.

She put both her elbows back on the table and said, "Look at me, boy. Put your hands up here and let me see your lines, and you consider my eyes." She studied my palm for a moment or two and said, "Umhmm, you have uncommon anguish for a boy."

She held my attention the whole time she was talking to me. It was hypnotic the way she paid attention to what she was saying. I couldn't wait to tell Claire about it.

"Listen closely," she told me. "We all experience low places in the road. You just have to endure some bumps in this life. The key to elevating your journey is figuring out how to change your course. And no matter how perilous things seem, find the courage to face trouble, boy. Once you find that in yourself, you'll understand what you gotta do. Dig deep, you have to forgive yourself and that anguish will dissipate. The true measure of a person is judged only by you and your maker." She put the palm of her hand over the top of my hat and pulled my face toward hers. "You're going to have to realize, my boy, that some people look at this world through the wrong end of the telescope." Then she got up and walked around me and took the hat off my head. When she touched my hair, I started to say something, but I stayed quiet instead.

The old lady put my hat back on my head and walked back to her chair. She slowly sat down, saying, "Time's up now, be on your way! Remember, boy, nobody but you know the measure of you."

Trust

Claire was waiting for me across the way by the House of Mirrors. As I walked up to her, she said, "What took you so long? Did you ask that old lady out on a date, or what?"

I faked a scowl. "Real funny, Claire." I looked at the House of Mirrors. "Don't tell me you want to go in here?"

"You don't like the Mirrors, Hats?" she said smartly, rolling her eyes.

I shook my head. "They make me dizzy, plus I'm still a little freaked out about the fortune lady."

Claire sighed and raised her right crutch into the air in disgust. "What the heck did that fraud tell you?"

"Did you see her eyes? They're white."

Sounding frustrated, Claire said, "Hats, she's a hundred and eight years old. Everything turns white. So, what?"

I shot back, "Well, what did she tell you?"

"Something from a thousand and one cliché's," she snapped. "Either that or something from old man Kim's fortune cookie bin."

She stopped walking and postured herself in front of me. "I suppose you got profound meaning from Miss Witchipoo?"

I shook my head. "Man, I thought I had a smart mouth. She made a lot of sense to me. That's all I'm saying. Something to think about, you know?"

Claire poked her bottom lip out and kind of flipped her hands forward as if to say, whatever you say.

I changed the subject. "Sweet Face, can you believe we haven't seen Piggyback out here today? He usually eats out here for ten days straight."

"I am surprised. He must have had something else going on," she agreed. "Hey Hats, you want to get a corndog?"

"Heck yeah!" Like frogs after the rain, the colored lights began to reveal themselves as daylight gave way to the night. Claire was heading straight for some tables that were bunched up together in a group. So, I suggested the obvious. "Hey, Sweet Face, let's go ahead and sit at one these picnic tables for a bit."

I looked across the table at my friend after we had eaten our food. As she brushed her hair back away from her face, I could see how hard she worked to conceal the fact that every step had been painful for her. Yet she was always worried about me. That was Claire, and this was our dance.

I reached for Claire's hand and gave it a squeeze saying, "Pretty long day, huh, Claire?"

"Yeah, I'm kind of worn out, Hats." She looked down at her crumpled napkin and said, "Listen, you trusted me talking about Abby, so I know I can tell you what that fortune lady told me."

She fidgeted with her napkin, looking nervous. Claire Hanover never looked nervous. But it didn't stop her talking. "I didn't want to say anything before, but that old lady kind of got under my skin too. Finn, she knew stuff I never told anybody. I've kept a journal ever since I learned to write, and she knew about that. She told me God gifts those who face the challenges they were born to. She said I haven't realized my gift yet and that I would bring change to people's lives with my words one day."

I looked at her like she had three eyeballs and asked, "What in the world are you talking about?"

She turned her head sideways like she always does when I'm supposed to understand without explanation. Then she said kind of slow-like, "Well, I wanna be a writer someday. And nobody but you have ever heard me say that. As a matter of fact, I wrote a poem about you last year after you gave your lunch money to that kid who had to give his up to the Garretts."

I looked at her in disbelief and said, "No, you did not."

"I most certainly did, Finn McCleary. I have it saved on my phone. You want to read it?"

Before I could answer, Claire tapped a few buttons on her phone and stretched her arm out in front of her, handing me the telephone. I hesitated to even look at the phone. I knew I wasn't going to handle this well. But it was too late now.

I took the phone and looked at the screen. Claire had written this long poem. And it was titled "Folded Umbrella." This was supposed to be about me? Weird. I'd read it and be nice.

Folded Umbrella

His rain is unsheltered

A stoic one certainly is he

While he fills the night with fears

He walks with purpose yet puts on no airs

His heart beats with the fury of a hundred lions

Though no one is there

There is a longing in the deep blue-green recess

That speaks only a whispered language

Lightly, nightly, to his ear

And one day this folded umbrella shall hear

Shall hear

There are those chosen few

Those gifted ones

With treasures in their hearts

Called from on high

Called to impart

These talents given you

To lift other hearts

Hear the whispers, folded umbrella

Unfold your heart

Release your supply

Give and you shall receive

Seek joy in all you do

The rain in your heart will forever dry...
Claire M. Hanover

I read every line and I just grinned. How could I read this and not smile? I mean it was almost like going to church. She watched my face as I read it, then said, "You liked it?" Her eyes brightened. "You liked it!"

"Well. . .sure I liked it. It's. . .you're. . .amazing.

She flashed a broad smile. "Good. That's. . .really good."

✱ ✱ ✱

It was a quiet drive to Claire's house. We both rode in the back, her crutches on the floorboard.

When we hit her driveway, I was so relaxed that the bump startled me. I looked over at Claire and her head was facing the other window. She was asleep. Another five minutes and I would have been too. I shook her shoulder and kind of whispered to her, "Claire, we're home."

She rubbed her owlet eyes and began blinking very

quickly. "Wow, I was out!" After she came to life a bit, she put her lips close to my ear and said quietly, " Remember what I said. About going to see your mom."

I nodded and forced a smile, then jumped out of the car, grabbed her crutches and ran around to help her get situated to walk up to her porch. Of course, she insisted that she didn't need help, but her arms were trembling on her crutches. I pretended not to notice as we said goodnight, but I worried all the way home.

A Long Time Coming

I got to the bus stop a little bit early and Claire was already there. I knew something was up because she was way too chipper this early.

"Good morning, Hats," she chirped. "How are you today?"

I gave her a wrinkled-nose look and said, "I'm okay, but what about you? "I'm fine, Finn. We're skipping school today." I started to protest, but she held up a hand. "Just listen please. You and I are going to walk two blocks down to the regular bus stop, and we're gonna ride over so you can go see your momma. I'll wait at the Starbucks across the street while you visit, but today's the day."

I stepped away from her and shook my head like I hadn't heard what I'd heard.

"You want me to skip school? Have you met my Dad? I don't think you've thought this through, Claire. I mean, I'm already down to one parent and when my dad finds out, he'll hang me up by my ears right before he sends me to military school."

Claire lifted her chin. "I think maybe you underestimate your dad, Finn. But if he finds out, I'll be glad to talk to him with you. I'll even say it was my idea. Come on, Finn. Let's do this. The bus will be there in fifteen minutes."

"This is crazy, Claire." The thought of seeing my mom made my stomach crawl all the way up to my throat. What if she didn't want to see me?

But what if she did? I had Googled her current address only a month or so ago, so it was kind of weird that Claire was pushing this.

I forced the hope back down. Better to expect the worst. Then I wouldn't be disappointed when she told me to hit the road.

I took in a deep breath and tried one last time. "She's probably not even home."

"Then we will have had a nice bus ride." The look in her eyes told me nothing I could say was going to change her mind.

For a moment, I stood there biting my lip while hope

battled it out with panic. Finally, my shoulders slumped. "Fine, but if we're going, let's go."

Luckily, we got away from our stop before the school bus got there, so no one was the wiser. By the time we arrived in the next town over, Crystal Bay, where my mother was living, I was a nervous wreck. I had never had the guts to make the trip before.

Her apartment was only a short walk from the bus stop. And just as Claire had said, there was a Starbucks right across the street. No surprise there. Claire loves Google maps. I looked over at my mom's apartment building. I kind of hated to just show up. Maybe she was still in bed. She'd always been an early riser, but maybe that had changed.

"You think we should call her first?" I said.

"It's too late to call," Claire said. "We're already here. Besides, if you call her first, you'll just find some excuse not to go inside."

We got off the bus and Claire pushed me in the right direction. "Now Finn, I'll be right across the street, and I've got my phone. Take all the time you need. My Mom knows what I'm doing today."

That settled it. One Hanover woman was a force of nature. Two were an act of God.

I took the elevator to the third floor of the old apartment building and walked down the dimly lit hall until I found the door that should have had the numbers 323 on it. But the numbers weren't there anymore. You could still make them out, because the wood where they used to be was lighter. I took a deep breath and knocked. Nothing. I put my ear to the door and tried to listen for voices. I couldn't hear a darn thing. I knocked four times. Nobody came to the door, and I knocked again, a little harder and a few more times. This time I heard a voice say, "All right, I'm comin'. Keep your shirt on."

The door opened slightly, but the chain stayed latched, and the mother I hadn't seen or spoken to in years peeked through the crack and said, "Whatever you're selling, I ain't buying."

"No, Ma'am, I—" And the door slammed shut.

Now that I was there, I wasn't about to give up that easily. I knocked with the side of my fist and said with as much courage as I could summon, "Hannah McCleary, I'm not a salesman. I'm your son. It's Finn McCleary."

How stupid was that? Like she didn't know her own son's name? But then, she hadn't recognized my face. The thought made my eyes burn, but I took a deep breath and said past the knot in my throat, "I'm not leaving until I talk to you. Mom, please open the door."

There wasn't a peep for at least a minute. I wondered if I'd still be standing there this time tomorrow morning. Claire would have to spend the night at Starbucks, and it would serve her right for getting me into this. Then I heard the chain being slowly taken loose, and shortly after that the door barely opened.

My Mom stood just inside it with her head down and her eyes looking up at me. Then her shoulders started to shake, and tears spilled down her face. She grabbed me and squeezed me so tight I could hardly breathe.

"Finny Joe, oh Finny Joe," she said between sobs. "Is it really you? You're so tall. I got a picture from your daddy but it's just not the same."

I hugged her back, and I thought I'd break her. She seemed so small.

"Mom, how do you feel? Are you better?"

"Oh, Finn." She took a deep breath and stepped out of my arms, hugging herself instead of me. "Why did you come here?"

Lifetime Movie

"Look at me," she said. "I'm just a ghost. They got me off the pills and now my hands shake so bad I have to use both to drink a cup of coffee."

She held them out to show me, then looked into my eyes. Slowly, her expression changed, as if she were just waking up. "Oh, honey. None of this is your fault. None of it. I'm the one who left."

She gestured for me to sit on the couch, then sank into the chair across the room and rubbed her upper arms like she was freezing. The words came out in a flood as she tried to make me understand that her leaving had nothing to do with Dad either. Losing Abigail broke her in a way that wasn't fixable. She felt like it wasn't fair to our family to drag us down just because she couldn't cope.

The longer I sat and listened to her talk, the weirder I felt. I thought I'd be upset but it was more like watching a Lifetime movie. Time had changed everything.

My mother had thick, shiny hair that dragged across my face when she kissed me goodnight. This lady's hair. . .Hannah's hair. . .was thin and stringy. And she sat way across the room from me like she was scared of me. My Mom would never have done that. It was clear to me that this was no longer my mother. She was just someone I used to know.

It wasn't her fault, but it made me feel sad. It was almost like I was burying someone who hadn't died.

"I never stopped loving you," she said. "You or your father. But I...didn't deserve you. You were better off without me."

"I love you too," I said, because it seemed like the right thing to say. "I'll pray for you. That you find peace in your heart. That you'll be. . .you know. . .okay." Deep down, I knew it was a long shot that I would ever even see this woman again.

As I walked out the door, Hannah hit me with a fastball right in the breadbasket. "Thanks for letting see how handsome you got, Idaho Kid."

With my back to her, for a moment, I was four years old again. It was all I could do not to run back and throw her over my shoulder and carry her home. But I knew it was way too late. So, I didn't look back. I just said, "Bye, Mom" over my shoulder and got out of there as fast as I could.

Claire and I hopped back on the bus. I was still worried about Dad finding out about all this. I did say a little prayer about not ending up in military school. I had a feeling a place like that would be full of Herschel Garrett types.

Dad got home an hour or so after I did, and he was in a good mood. Thank you, Lord.

First thing out of his mouth was, "How was school, Bud?"

I shrugged. "School's always the same, Dad."

"You okay, Finn?"

"Yes Sir."

"You sure? You sound a little. . .off."

"I'm kinda tired. Long day."

"All right, Bud, turn on the tube. I'm gonna get a Coke from the fridge. Want one?"

"Sure, Dad."

In one horrifying second, I realized what an idiot I was. I had emptied my pockets out, like I always do, on the table beside the refrigerator. The ticket stub from the Greyhound bus was in my pocket and had a stamp with Crystal Bay bigger than life on it. He was going to walk right by it twice in the next twenty seconds.

From the kitchen, my Dad yelled, "Hey, Finn."

I'm dead, I thought to myself.

"Yes Sir."

"You want a glass or not?"

"No Sir, I'll just drink it out of the bottle."

I couldn't believe he didn't bust me. His eyes must really be going. Thank you, God above. I was sweating bullets. Then Dad said, "Well Bud, I made you a plate. It's in the microwave. I'm beat, gonna turn in early tonight. Goodnight."

"K, thanks. Night, Dad."

I pumped my fist in the air as his bedroom door closed behind him. I was home free!

The Bus

The next Monday, I nearly broke a sweat getting to the bus stop and I just knew I was gonna get wet. It was dark as night. My alarm clock didn't go off again, so I was running late. If not for the thunder, I would have slept all day. And of course, as soon as I got there, I was reminded of the obvious by my dear friend, Claire.

"You're late, buddy boy."

"Hey, why are you out here, Sweet Face? You're never on time to the stop."

"I know, but I got rested up yesterday."

"I noticed. We missed you at church."

"I was so tired, Hats. I slept and slept and slept."

"Well, you must have needed it. Feel better now?" A drop of rain splatted on my forehead.

"Much." As more drops fell, Claire inched up toward the curb and steadied her crutches. "Here comes Mister Red." I held my book bag just over our heads to block the rain as we headed for the bus.

You could hear the chatter from the bus before Mr. Red even hit the squeaky brakes. Our bus was loaded with kids that weren't usually on there with us.

Sweet Face and I hesitantly boarded the bus. I always went in behind her in case she needed a boost. Once we were on level landing she asked Mr. Red, "What in the world is going on today?"

He mopped his sweaty forehead with his sleeve and said, "I had to pick up an extra route at Bonner Pass, Honey-bunch. Their driver is out today."

Claire looked back at me with a curled lip and said, "Bonner Pass, Ugh! Of all places." She wasn't kidding. You'd be crazy to go to Bonner Pass after dark without a bulletproof vest and a combination lock on your wallet.

As Claire passed him, Mr. Red and I exchanged shots from our finger guns. Maybe I was imagining things, but his draw seemed a little slow.

Ignoring our antics, Claire said, "Hats, will you walk in front of me and see if you can find us a seat?"

"Okay, I'll find one. Stay close to me so your crutches don't catch. It's so crowded in here."

About four seats back, Herschel Garrett was just waiting for us to get on so he could say something regrettable. I had just walked past him, for obvious reasons, and I heard his voice.

I turned as he was talking to Claire and this look came over her face that I've seen so many times. It was like she had accidently drank vinegar. And I thought, oh my God, Herschel, I feel sorry for you. His mistake was talking to her at all, much less saying, "Hiya, Hot Stuff. I saved you a seat. Why don't you rest your crippled self, right here in my lap?"

Without pause, Claire fired back, "Stick your leg out here, Herschel. By the time I'm done beatin' you with this crutch, you'll be the only cripple on this bus."

One thing no one would ever say about Claire Hanover was that she was ever at a loss for words.

Herschel's leer practically stretched his face in two. "C'mon, Honey, I know you missed me."

"You must wanna wear my breakfast, you mutant gorilla."

I didn't see any reason for her to go to prison over this modern-day Goliath, so I grabbed her arm and said, "Ignore him, Claire. Come back here. I've got us a spot behind Oliver. Hand me your crutches. I'll put them in the aisle for you."

I thought I was gonna have to gag Claire, because she kept on about Herschel. "He thinks he's God's gift. Let me give him a piece of my mind. He's not gonna talk to me that way."

I mean, he got way under her skin. Which was unusual. Finally, she pulled herself around and swung into a place holding the back of the seat in front of her, then firmly sitting with a giant sigh.

She apologized to Oliver, sitting in front of

her, whose shoulder she momentarily grabbed trying to maintain her balance.

Fortunately, there were only two more stops made before we headed for Washout Road. And the last pickup was none other than the Eyebrow himself, Tommy Slater. He and his long legs sat on the tiny seat right behind the driver. I think it was the last available place on the bus.

It had begun to rain really hard outside.

By the time we got to the cutoff to Washout Road, it was raining sheets, and when you looked out the window you could hardly even see the tree line. There was a good reason this road had a descriptive name. It was wide, made of dirt and rock and graded on a steep angle to the right.

Occasionally, the bus would catch water and the tail end would jackknife just a bit and then bite ground again. My heart jumped every time it happened.

As we turned off the highway onto Washout, I noticed the bus lunging and braking several times like we were running out of gas.

And then we just began to coast down the road at a pretty slow speed. Claire was the first one to notice Mister Red. She grabbed her crutches out of the aisle and started screaming to the kids in her way. "Clear the middle, something's wrong."

Mr. Red had slid way down in his seat and had only one hand on the wheel. His lips were moving soundlessly, and his face looked as white as chalk.

"Move, please," I said to Oliver and his sister Rachel. "Move!"

We were slowly heading toward the edge of this old road, with the Grand River a sixty foot drop off the shoulder, and only a small metal rail between us and it. As the bus headed down the steep grade, our wheels began to slide toward the river. Through windows sheeted with rain, I caught glimpses of rock and brush and the sheer drop beyond.

A couple of kids screamed, and Herschel clenched his knees to his chest and said, over and over, "We're gonna die! We're gonna die because of that goofy old man!" I could hear him over the others because his voice, unlike mine and most of the others, had made it through puberty already.

Mr. Red moaned. In a last gasp of hope, he wrenched the steering wheel around. The bus spun to the left. A couple of kids screamed as a rear wheel dipped, then leveled. The kids had glued themselves to the windows on each side of the bus like human flies, trying to figure out what was going on. They kept having to clear the fog off the windows with their forearms to see out.

Before any of us could get to the front of the bus, we hit some big bumps and then came to a sudden stop that jolted everyone forward. Mr. Red had managed to negotiate the bus far enough away from the river to coast us into a big rocky area that had landed this missile. We were all rocked around but none of us were seriously hurt. Scared half to death, but at least we weren't plummeting anymore. The rain sounded like a drum machine on the metal top.

Nobody cheered when we stopped short of the edge. Instead, there was the strangest kind of silence. It was like we had all been holding our breath for a really long time and we could finally breathe. But we were still scared to move.

Claire made her way to Mister Red, but she had to squeeze her skinny legs in behind his seat and reach over the metal bar to reach him because he had fallen over toward his window. She had gone with her mom lots of times on the weekend for her home health job, so she knew what to do. Claire took Mr. Red's pulse, then swung herself around the bar and began CPR on him, propping herself against the steering wheel.

While I fought my way to the front of the bus, she did rescue breathing on Mister Red for what seemed like a long time, then checked his pulse again. "Crap!" she shouted, then clamped her mouth shut. Her chin quivered.

I knelt on the top step just to the right side of the driver seat and said, "Is he dead?"

She said with a clenched fist, "Not yet."

Then in front of God and thirty-seven witnesses, Claire took the side of her fist and hit Mr. Red harder than any girl I've ever seen. Right in the chest. I didn't look, but I swear she knocked the hair off Mr. Red's chest. And to the shock of everyone, he let out a long gasp for air that sounded just like Frankenstein.

"Jesus, Mary and Joseph!" I said, and clapped my hand over my mouth. Apparently, the stress of the situation had turned me into my father.

I looked out the top part of the bus door. The guardrail was only feet away. I started to shiver.

I think nearly everybody on the bus made a 911 call at some point during this roller coaster ride, so it wasn't long before Emergency services arrived and took Mr. Red to the hospital. The rest of us were unharmed and brought to school. By a tow truck, no less. Geez Louise!

Grace

By the time we made it to Ms. Meadows classroom, the hall was abuzz about the bus accident. And who else but Piggyback Kidd was leading the investigation. As soon as he saw me, he hot-footed it over and began killing my ear.

"Hats, I heard, man. The one time I don't ride, this goes down. Are you serious? Tell me everything. Was it drastic or what? You okay?"

I just wasn't in the mood. It wasn't his fault, but I cut him off. "After class, Piggyback. It's time for the second bell. I'm fine but Mr. Red's in the hospital. That's all that really matters, man."

I hurried into the classroom, a sick feeling in the pit of my stomach. It was partly worry for Mr. Red and partly worry about the partner project. I might have been the only one whose mother had checked out, but I knew I wasn't the only one who dreaded this assignment. Doing research—or anything else, for that matter—with a subhuman degenerate like Herschel Garrett could only have detrimental outcomes, in my estimation. And I was still a little shaken up about how close we'd come to dying in a fiery crash. Or a rainy crash. Whatever.

We'd decided our foursome would include Eugenia and Claire, who might make things at least bearable. I thought it would be mature to swallow my pride and sit near Herschel. I would speak to him before we were turned loose on our projects.

What was I thinking?As the rest of the class filed into the room, I leaned over and tapped Herschel on the back. He half turned around, and I said, "You got a blank piece of paper I can borrow?"

I just wanted to see how he was gonna act toward me. He turned away again and mumbled, "I ain't got no paper."

I got up and went back to my regular seat. I thought to myself, this project is going to be all on me. But if that was how it was going to be, I'd be darned if his name was going on it. What a jerk.

Ms. Meadows came in looking kind of subdued and gave us a few minutes to write get-well notes for Mr. Red. She stood in front of her desk and cleared her throat to speak. "Class, I want to say just a word or two about the accident. I know several of you were in the wreck and are okay, thankfully."

It was clear that Ms. Meadows was trying hard not to cry, and she was holding it together well as she continued to speak. "I'm told that Mr. Red is going to be okay as well, after some well-deserved rest."

A few kids sniffled and wiped their eyes, and I couldn't help but notice no one was laughing at Old Mr. Red now.

When we turned in our notes, she sent us right into our groups. Claire, Eugenia and I pushed our desks into kind of a triangle. Captain personality started out near the group and inched his way back toward the rear of the room.

We had a list of historical figures to choose from to do research on. Hershel made it very clear that he didn't care who I picked. He tried to get Ms.

Meadows to let him go to the nurse, but she didn't bite. She did let him go the bathroom, though. He didn't come back.

I decided to do a report on Napoleon. There was a whole chapter in our textbooks on him that we hadn't covered. I told Claire I was going to sit behind them and read so she and Eugenia could get started on theirs.

But it was hard to concentrate. Thoughts of Mom kept creeping in. I shook my head. I didn't want to think about my mother. Why had Claire made me go and see her anyway?

I pushed the thoughts of my mother away and focused on watching the girls in front of me. Eugenia would touch Claire's hair and ask, "Do you dye your hair this color?" and "How do you get it so soft?"

Claire didn't like it a bit. She said angrily, "No I don't dye my hair. Are you crazy?" She slapped Eugenia's hand away. "Quit touching me. I don't even know you, Eugenia."

Eugenia put both her hands underneath her legs

and looked down in embarrassment. "Sorry, I just like your hair."

"Forget it," Claire muttered.

Eugenia perked up and asked, "Claire, do you have any sisters?"

"No, I don't," Claire said, sounding annoyed. "Let's just pick a subject for our project, okay?"

I read about half my chapter, but I think I read every page twice because I was paying more attention to Claire and Eugenia.

It fascinated me that Claire was pulling this off with the female version of Herschel and I couldn't even keep my partner in the room.

Eugenia asked Claire if she had a choice out of the list that Ms. Meadows gave them.

Claire took the list in her hand and held it in front of her. She said, "Well, there are a couple that I think are good choices."

Eugenia cocked her head and asked, "Do you feel strongly about any of them?"

"Strongly, no." Claire frowned at the list, then looked up at Eugenia. "Why, do you?"

Eugenia grinned broadly. "Yes, there's only one choice for me. I want to pick Joan of Arc, if it's okay with you. I'd like to know more about her relationship with Noah."

Claire looked dumbfounded and said, "I think you misunderstand. Never mind. We'll research everything we can about Joan together, all right? It's a good idea you had."

I was sitting there pretending to read. And I could hardly believe my eavesdropping ears. This goth-looking, low-rent thug of a semi-girl was sounding a little bit human.

Claire gave Eugenia a speculative look and said, "You want to ask Ms. Meadows if we can go to the library and check out some books to use for references?"

Eugenia hopped up, smiled big, and said, "Sure." Then she hit Claire in the arm like a boy. Eugenia headed toward the teacher's desk and Claire glared at me and rubbed her arm. Then she rolled her eyes and held her palms in front of her, like she was saying, *what do I do?*

But I had already failed babysitting bullies 101, so I shrugged and said out loud, "Beats me, Claire."

When Eugenia got back to her desk, she sat down easy. She looked at Claire, who was straightening her papers and putting them back in her folder.

"Ms. Meadows will let us use the library tomorrow," she said. "She said today was just for topic discussion."

Their desks were still facing one another kind of at an angle and Eugenia reached to touch Claire's hand. "Please don't slap me. I want to ask you something." She pulled her hand back and said, "Do you think you could do me a big favor?"

Warily, Claire replied, "I guess so. What?"

Eugenia looked down at her hands, then said in a small voice, "My middle name is Grace. That's what my Momma calls me. The school's always called me Eugenia 'cause it's on the rolls that way. And

I guess it fits my looks. Plus, having a sister people call Bulldog don't help none. But I go by Grace at home. You think maybe you could call me that?"

Claire's eyebrows shot up and her mouth gaped open.

"That's not the easiest request," she said. "I mean, I am kind of used to calling you Eugenia, but . . . Well, I guess, if anybody understands being called names they're not comfortable with, it would be me. So, I'll give it a try, Eugenia. Sorry, I mean, Grace." Then she rubbed her arm again and added, "But can we agree, at least while we're partners, no hitting?"

With a solemn expression, Eugenia Grace said, "Yeah, I'll do my best."

Now I've heard some crazy things in my life. But after listening in on the conversation between my friend Claire and the prizefighter formerly known as Eugenia Rojas, I had plans to have my ears examined by a licensed professional, pronto.

And then everyone was saved by the bell. Before

we escaped, Ms. Meadows pleaded, "Straighten the desks before you leave, please."

I wanted to confirm with Claire that I'd heard what I heard, but as soon as we all headed for the door, Eugenia pinned me by the chalkboard so no one else could hear and said, "I don't know how much you heard, but I know you were listening, so here's the deal. What's between me and Claire stays that way. *Capiche*, Hat boy?"

A Man Called Ethan

Mornings in my house were nearly all the same. At least during the week, I mean. Today was no different. I was up after I had hammered my alarm clock a good three times.

I threw on some clothes and stumbled to the bathroom, then looked in the mirror. My hideous hair was even worse than usual. It looked like a cornered porcupine. No way could I go into Ms. Meadows' classroom looking like this.

I filled the sink with water and buried my head in it, hoping to just wet it down. When I came out of the sink like my dog Gus comes out of a bath, instead of slicking down, my hair bounced right up like a springboard diving champion. A strange, high-pitched, girl-like noise escaped from my mouth. I didn't know my voice went that high. I was used to bad hair days, but this was ridiculous. I tried brushing it, combing it, putting goop in it. Nothing helped at all.

I looked in the mirror and thought about how pretty my sister had been and how much my mom had loved dressing her in lacy clothes and brushing her perfect little curls. No wonder my mom had left. I wondered if she wished it had been me who drowned. I just started grabbing stuff from the counter and throwing it. I was so mad.

I banged into the wall behind me and afterward heard the crash in my bedroom. I ran into the hall, and back into my room, to see my framed poster of Derek Jeter on the floor with the glass broken.

Then it hit me. I wasn't mad because of my hair. I wasn't even mad about my mom. Well, I was, but not mad enough to trash our bathroom. I was still mad about yesterday and how I didn't get to talk to Claire. Claire and I always talk about everything. And between the visit to my mother, the bus wreck, and what had happened with Eugenia, there was a lot to talk about.

All the mad bled out of me, and in its place, I felt only a kind of hollow sadness. I bent to pick up the poster and suddenly I heard my Dad's voice from the kitchen. "Finn Joseph, what's going on in there?"

He must have heard me making all the racket. Oh God! I was getting middle named. And first thing in the morning. Just take me now, Jesus.

Before I could gather myself, he was standing there with his big red Irish face in the crack of the door. He knocked two quick taps on the door and said, "What in hell fire, boy? It sounds like a wrecking crew in here this morning."

Without waiting for me to answer, dad slowly pushed the door open enough to see that the bathroom was a disaster. The lines around his mouth went tight, and he slowly looked around the room.

My Dad was one of those kinds of guys who expected explanations before he started asking for them. I knew I better hit the gas on giving him one. "I got a little upset about my hair, Dad. I'm sorry."

I was steadily picking things up off the floor as I was apologizing, hoping for better results. My Dad sighed heavily. He began to rub his forehead and play with his mustache, watching without a word as I cleaned the bathroom. Dad looked down at me as I got the last of my fit off the floor and he said, "Let's go in the kitchen and think about this before you go to school."

I didn't remember seeing him look this disappointed in a long time. I didn't understand what the big deal was. I got a little irate in the john. I apologized. Come on.

He began by saying, "Finn, I know things haven't been easy for you, son. And I probably could have handled some things differently. But we're all given situations to deal with. You're a young man now. Son, temper tantrums are for babies and don't solve a thing."

God, was I ready to shave my head now. A lecture before school, Geez Louise! He gestured for me to sit down and started making breakfast while he talked. I swear, sometimes my father talks to me the same way he did when I ran around with Mercurochrome-painted knees.

He cracked an egg into a bowl and said, "Now, I

know you have this thing with your hair. But the sooner you accept who you are and what you are as a person, the better off you're going to be. I thought you were past this vanity stuff since you started wearing those hats. Did you know that your mother had to fight guys off with a stick before we got married? And that's who you get your hair from."

"Yeah, Dad, but hers is straight not wild, thick and bushy."

"Are you having a hard time dealing with what happened on the bus?"

"No, Dad, I'm fine."

"Having trouble with your classes or that new teacher? What's her name, Miller?"

I didn't want to tell him how Ms. Meadows wouldn't let me wear my hat in class, and I couldn't very well tell him I'd gone to see Mom, could I? As conclusively as I knew how, I said, "No Dad, school is fine. My teacher's name is Meadows and I like her okay. I just woke up frustrated this morning. Period, end of story. I'm sorry, and I'll try to do better, honest."

He went on as if he hadn't heard me. "I want to tell about a man I used to know in the war."

"Oh, Dad, I'm gonna be late for school," I complained and laid my head on the kitchen table. I respect my Dad, I really do, but war stories are the worst.

My Dad wasn't having it, though. He cracked another egg and said, "I'll write you a note. This is important. Now sit up and listen."

I had to interrupt, or I'd never get to school. "Dad, I have to finish getting ready, but I can hear you from my room."

"Stay right where you are." He waited until I sank back into my chair, then said, "You remember me telling you about when I was in Afghanistan?"

"Yes Sir," I mumbled.

"Well, when I was there each of us in my outfit had partners. We called them blankets. A blanket's job in a combat situation was to protect his partner from enemy fire and help provide warmth in a foxhole. My blanket and I were together on twenty-nine missions. His name was Ethan Mann and he was from Kentucky."

"Dad, seriously. I'm gonna be late. You don't have to fix breakfast. I'm not even hungry."

He tossed me the bread and nodded toward the toaster. I sighed and got up to make the toast. When he got his mind set on something, there was no changing it.

Dad whisked the eggs together and poured them into a skillet, then continued his story while I got out the butter and waited for the toast.

"As I was saying, when Ethan was nine years old, he worked in the summer for his grandfather on a big horse farm. Ethan loved the horses. There was one quarter horse that he had become attached to since it was a colt. But he wasn't allowed to ride the high dollar horses. These horses were raised to race and be track run only."

I was tempted to interrupt my Dad again, but the tone of his voice had changed, and I didn't feel like I was being lectured any longer. I sat and waited for him to tell me this piece of his history.

But now that I was ready to hear it, Dad was in no hurry. He finished the eggs and plopped them onto a couple of plates. They smelled great.

I dug in, but Dad didn't eat his. Instead he paced around the table back and forth to the window like he was expecting someone. Pivoting away from the window, my Dad finished telling the tale of his friend with his hands laced behind his neck.

"One August evening after Ethan's grandfather found out that he had secretly ridden this horse in a grass field, he took Ethan behind one of the barns and beat him with a buggy whip. He was beaten from behind, but the long whip wrapped around and caught his face. He was left with a deep scar from the corner of his right eye to the edge of his mouth.

"Here's the thing, Finny Joe. Ethan was a good-looking guy, but you could hardly stand to look at him. One hot miserable day in the Middle East, Ethan and I were scouting a side street where some

Afghan children were playing. It was a narrow street between two buildings. You wouldn't believe the heat over there, Finn. Just as I was wiping sweat from my eyes, one of those kids yelled, 'Hey Johnny!'"

Dad took in a long breath. His hands tightened on the back of his neck. "They were always yelling at us, so I don't know why that day was any different but for a millisecond, I half-glanced backward. We were trained to ignore distractions and I didn't do it that day. Before I even had time to look back around, Ethan shoved me sideways against the stone building so hard that I fell backward to the ground." He paused, looking off into the distance, like he could see it happening right in front of him. "I actually felt a rush of anger that he shoved me like that. But it only lasted a second, because when he shoved me, he fell across a trip wire that was connecting the buildings. A bomb exploded, blasting him and that terrible scar right off the planet."

I laid my fork back on the table. Suddenly I really wasn't hungry anymore.

Dad said softly, "You see, it's not the package were wrapped in that's important. And it's not only what's inside. What's important, what's really important, is what we decide to do with what we're given. I think you're old enough to understand these things, Finn. And I know you're smart enough. I know I don't say it enough, but I am proud of you." He looked at me again and, even though it was totally not possible, it was like he knew all the stuff I wasn't telling him. "Do you get the meaning of what I'm telling you, son?"

"Yes Sir, I think I do, Dad." I answered. It was a great story, I had to admit. But I wasn't sure how I felt about it. If not for this Ethan guy, I wouldn't have a Dad. I wouldn't even be me.

Dad looked at his watch and suddenly he was in a hurry, rushing around gathering change and his keys. "Get your hat, buddy. We gotta go."

I had to remind him that I still had stuff to do. "I just have to feed Gus real quick. I'll meet you at the car. Hey Dad, did you write my note yet?"

"Doing it right now, buddy," he said and reached

into the kitchen drawer for a pad and pen.

I grabbed a hat, stuck it in my bag and ran out to feed Gus. I couldn't stop thinking about Ethan and his terrible scar. If maybe he'd thrown himself at that trip-wire, so he'd never have to see that scar again, or if he'd simply saved his friend without thinking, because that was what men did. They saved their friends. I wondered how it felt to be my dad and know you were still here because somebody else wasn't.

It felt weird, but I also couldn't stop smiling. This was the best talk I'd had with my dad in a long time.

The Pep Rally

One thing that had slipped my mind until right before we left the house was that we had a pep rally scheduled for today. This meant that all my friends could sit together and act crazy practically all afternoon. We just had to survive the classes up to lunch. That was a piece of cake.

By the time I made it to school, I was good and late. Fortunately, a written excuse from a parent was enough to pacify most teachers. The morning grind flew by and all my friends were looking forward to a relaxing afternoon in the school gym at the pep rally. This rally was for the boys' basketball team. But that was secondary to the fact that everyone got out of class half a day and could yell and scream without getting in trouble. We all thought this was a grand concept.

In the cafeteria during lunch, we had what Piggyback called a "war room meeting" to discuss girls. The whole gang was there. I got there a little late because I had to turn in some extra credit work for English. Apparently Piggyback had already gotten ribbed hard for slobbering over some girl a year younger than us.

Claire was ready to condemn our whole process of female worship. "Why do you boys have to sit around and pretend these girls are something that they aren't? And you never do anything about it. You just salivate. God, it's nauseating."

Thankfully the lunch bell was sounding, which meant it was time to head to the gym. Claire, Vinny, Piggyback, Tommy, and I all left the lunch room about the same time. As we headed out, a couple of kids gave Claire high fives for saving Mr. Red. She blushed and grinned, then punched Piggyback in the arm when he teased her about being a celebrity.

We didn't like to be the first ones in the gym because we always sat near the bottom of the bleachers for Claire's sake. And if you do that early, everyone steps all over you going up.

Since the gym was across the parking lot, I lagged back a bit with Claire. It took a few minutes to walk it and a little longer if you were on crutches like Claire. She and I hadn't talked much in the last couple of days, so I figured, no time like the present.

"Hadn't seen much of you lately," I said sort of jokingly.

"I know, you mad at me?" She sounded serious.

"Mad? Of course not."

We were walking very slowly toward the gym as if we both wanted to stop and talk instead. I knew we couldn't. Not now, anyway. But Claire surprised me by stopping and propping herself sideways on her crutches. "I missed talking to you. That's not usually the way we do it. I'll be home tonight. Will you please call me so that we can really talk?"

I touched her arm and nodded. "Definitely."

As we got nearer to the gym doors, there were only a few students gathering. We were early after all. We had a procedure that made things go a little smoother. While the guys saved our seats in the bleachers, I carried Claire's crutches into the gym because it was easier for her to use the hand rails that led to the front door instead of her crutches. Once inside, Claire could negotiate herself by just holding onto the bleachers themselves. We always sat in the first section, so she didn't have to go very far.

Piggyback saw Claire and me beside the bleachers, and he came to help her around the corner.

"Hey guys, I've got our regular seats right down there." He pointed proudly. As he and Claire got to their seats, I said, "I don't see Vinny. I'm gonna go check really quick and see if he's outside."

I looked around the front of the gym. No Vinny. I nearly fell down the steps because I was still carrying Claire's crutches. I don't know why I didn't leave them. I hurried back inside and just as I got onto the wooden part of the basketball court, someone yelled, "Hey, McWeirdo!"

I knew the voice without seeing the face. I didn't have a second to react before something crashed into me from behind. My legs flew out from under me like toppling bowling pins. My hat flew off my head and my hair sprang out. And Claire's crutches shot up like two bottle rockets headed for the moon. I slid on my back across that waxed floor, past the microphone stand where no one was standing yet. I reached out and grabbed the stand as I slowed down and rolled over to sit up. I was dazed but not so much that I couldn't make out Herschel Garrett and one of his buddies slinking away laughing.

I knew it was only a matter of minutes before the coaches came out and the pep rally began, and a strange idea started forming in my mind. I was going to get up and say something to these kids. Right here, right now. Maybe it was my dad's story that gave me the idea.

I climbed up the microphone stand and got my legs under me. Then I made eye contact with Piggyback, who was giving me the *do you need help* look. I held my hand up to him, so he'd know I was all right. As I turned the microphone switch on, I glanced at the crowd and noticed that only about half the bleachers were filled. It was still early, so I'd make this quick.

"Excuse me, everybody. My name is Finn McCleary. I know you guys saw what just happened to me. That kind of thing has been going on for a long time. And until now I never said anything about it." I paused to gather my thoughts. "But wrong is wrong. I learned something from my dad this morning. He says, it really doesn't matter who you are or what you look like. What's important, what's really important, is what we decide to do with the gifts that we are given. And we all have gifts. I didn't believe that before, but I believe him now. Some things must change, though. I wanna take this opportunity to thank Herschel Garrett for knocking some sense into me. Wherever you're hiding, Herschel, thanks a million. And thank ya'll for listening."

I stood there for a moment, my heart pounding like it was about to bust out of my chest.

Then from the corner of the gym someone whistled in appreciation and then a smattering of applause led by Claire and Piggyback followed. The whistler was Skinny Vinny, who had made it to the pep rally but was sitting right outside the visitor's dressing room. I knew Coach Baker must have made him sit there. He was in trouble for something. I figured he skipped P.E. again.

But I didn't have much time to think about it, because just then, the whole crowd was on its feet, clapping and whooping and stomping. On the front row, Claire had the biggest smile.

Herschel Garrett had stepped from the shadow of the bleachers. He was scowling, and I knew he'd find a way to make me suffer for this. But for the first time in my life, I didn't even care.

The Breezeway

Following the excitement at the pep rally, I spent nearly the entire evening on the telephone with each of my friends. I liked to talk, but I rarely spent much time on the phone, so my dad accused me of having a secret girlfriend that I didn't want him to know about.

"Seriously, Dad, there's no line forming anywhere over these looks." I said, as I jazz-handed my face. I was smiling inside, though, glad he was starting to joke around again.

My friends all had very supportive stuff to say when they called, and I was glad to hear it. I was a little surprised at their different versions, though. I thought Piggyback knew me better than to think I wanted to run for student council. But that's what he thought my intentions were. And Vinny, he acted like he was about as deep as a mud puddle, but he seemed to understand precisely what point I was making or at least attempting to. My friends are great. Very different, but great.

I got to thinking about how excited it made me when those kids in the stands stood up and clapped for what I said. And then I remembered just last summer when I went on a hot streak at the plate and went ten for eighteen. I got pretty darned excited about that too.

But it seems like there's always another shoe waiting to drop with me. I struck out seven times in a row after that hitting streak, so I was a little leery about what might come next. I call it caution. My dad calls me a worry wart. Don't know which one of us is right on this subject. Probably not me.

The next morning started normally. Thank goodness. I got through the first couple of classes perfectly fine. As a matter of fact, everyone seemed to be a little bit more friendly than usual.

I liked to cut through the office from second period to the breezeway to get to the science building. I don't even know why they call it the science building. Most of our classes are in that building and only one of them is a science class. But that's teachers for you.

As I was going through the front office toward the breezeway, Veronica Marsh turned around right in front of me. Veronica Marsh never got within five feet of me a day in my life. She is Mr. Rite's student office assistant and, oh my God, she was put together like a showroom Ferrari. Too perfect to breathe on. I looked up at her and I was hypnotized. I walked toward her and tripped on a computer cord on the floor and lost my balance. I fell forward and landed face first right on Veronica's chest, pushing her against the wall.

I immediately jumped backward as if I'd landed on a cactus. "I am so sorry and so clumsy, Veronica. Are you okay? Let me help you up."

She was laughing the whole time. "It's you", she said.

"What do you mean?" I asked.

"You're the guy that took on Garrett at the pep rally."

I couldn't keep myself from grinning. "Well, I wouldn't exactly say that."

"Yeah, you're that guy at the gym. What was your name again?"

I cleared my throat, like I had some confidence. But, truth be known, my tongue felt as thick as my foot. I couldn't even think straight.

"I'm Finn. Finn McCleary. But my friends call me Fats, I mean Hats. I gotta get to class, Veronica. Really sorry about crashing into you."

I couldn't get out of that office fast enough.

As I made my way into the breezeway, a scream from the left side of the brick pillars made me forget all about Veronica. It sounded like Claire.

I threw my book bag against the wall and ran toward her voice. I couldn't see her right away because kids were everywhere. As I pushed my way through and rounded the corner, I saw Claire trapped against a wall of lockers just down from the breezeway opening to the library. The two younger Garrett brothers, Marshall and Willard, had thrown her crutches to the ground and were towering over her, holding her wrists behind her. Their leader, Herschel, was nowhere to be seen, but there was no doubt that this was payback aimed at me.

As I ran closer, Vinny was running up from the opposite direction. He looked livid, with his face all red and his eyes bugged out. I felt livid too, because you could hear her scream across that whole side of the school and nobody was doing a thing about it. All these kids just watching like a car wreck.

I wanted to get to Claire. Vinny wanted to get to those hyenas. The people wouldn't get out of my way. Vinny was shouting, "Move, I'm comin' through! Let her go, Willard. Right now. One warning's all you get."

And he wasn't kidding. He and I went straight in at the same time, but he did the damage. I was reaching for Claire. Without her crutches or these animals holding her up, I knew she'd fold like a cheap suit.

Vinny Deluchi was skinny but he was fearless and strong. He grabbed Willard Garrett's shirt and slung him around against those lockers like a rag doll, yelling only inches from Willard's face, "If you ever touch this girl again, I swear to God!"

As soon as he realized his brother was in trouble, Marshall bolted off like he was on fire. I finally reached Claire. She was crying hard, her back to the lockers and both hands pinned to the sides of her head as she held onto a combination lock for dear life. I leaned in as she fell forward into me.

I caught her at the waist and eased her down to the floor. She wrapped her arms around my neck like a baby octopus. I didn't think she'd ever let go.

"Hey," I said. "It's okay. I'm gonna get you a chair from the library."

She shook her head and held on harder. "Stay here, Hats," she pleaded, wiping tears from her eyes. "Sit with me on the floor?"

So that's what I did. I sat with Claire while Vinny propped her crutches against the wall and then went to get Mrs. Banks, the nurse.

Claire was hugging so tightly I could hardly breathe. I put my arm around her and she started to tell me what had happened before we got there. We sat on the floor off to the side of the breezeway.

Claire loosened her grip a little. "Thank goodness you and Vinny came when you did. Those creeps would not let me go. I was waiting for you as usual. And I started to head toward the office and Marshall popped out from nowhere and he grabbed me. Scared me to death, Finn. I pulled away and swung my other crutch at him. I hit him right in the head. But it didn't stop him."

I had to stop her right there. "You hit Marshall Garrett in the head with your crutch?" I asked in disbelief.

"Uh, he was trying to hold me hostage. What would you suggest I do?"

"I don't know. I'm just glad you're okay." What a firecracker this girl was.

She flicked her hair out of her face, sighed

deeply and said, "I'm glad that's over. Thanks for being here for me."

I had this strange feeling of guilt for dive-bombing Veronica Marsh earlier. I didn't really know why. Seemed I didn't know a lot these days. My life seemed to be getting more and more confusing.

The nurse finally checked Claire out and said she'd be fine. But she did go home for the rest of the day. She had some bruises and a cut on her shin.

Just as Vinny and I were about to go to class, Claire's mom showed up. I ran over and gave her a hug.

Mrs. Hanover nearly always wore her hair in long black braids. She had the smoothest looking skin ever. It was the color of walnut varnish.

Claire's mom was from the Caribbean islands originally. She had a slight British accent that sounded so cool. She met Claire's dad overseas where he was stationed in the service. He died in some maneuver accident when Claire was little but that's all I know about him. I was always too uncomfortable to ask.

She asked me right away, "Is she okay, Finn?"

I said, "She's shaken up, Mrs. Hanover, but you know our Claire. Tough as a boot. Come this way."

I led her over to Claire, who looked up and said, "Hi Momma. I'm all right."

As her mother led her to the car, Claire turned back and called Vinny over. She grabbed his face with both hands and kissed him on the cheek. "You're a good friend to me, Vinny Deluchi."

In true Vinny form, he replied, "F'get about it, Sweet Face. You know you're aces wit' me."

Good Guys on Trial

Ms. Meadows had just about pulled off the perfect lullaby symphony with that silver pointer of hers. If not for the tap, tap, tapping of South America on the big plastic map, I'd have made it to the world series of dreams for sure. Just as my cheek was about to slip off the heel of my hand, I felt a sharp poke to my ribcage. Claire was trying to get my attention and had stabbed me with her crutch tip.

I said "Oh!" out loud.

Ms. Meadows called me out. "Yes, Mr. McCleary, do you have a comment?"

Now off guard twice, I coughed to try to cover and said, "No, ma'am, just something caught in my throat." When Ms. Meadows had turned back to the map, I looked at Claire and whispered, "I'm gonna kill you."

She looked at me seriously and said, "I hear Mr. Rite coming down the hall." Sure enough, there was no mistaking that sound. His big clown shoes sounded like a Clydesdale coming every time. Claire looked worried. "I know it's about yesterday," she whispered.

"Don't worry," I told her. "It'll be okay."

Ten seconds later, three knocks on the door and the big oaf himself burst in, exclaiming, "Excuse me, Ms. Meadows, but I need Vincent Deluchi, Finn McCleary and Claire Hanover to come with me, please."

Ms. Meadows complied like a good little soldier. "Okay, guys, you heard Mr. Rite. Get your books and follow the principal."

Why did I feel like we were going to jail? Where were the Garrett boys? We did the right thing and we were going to the principal's office?

We got to the outer office area and Mr. Rite took Vinny in by himself first. After a few minutes, Vinny came stomping out and threw himself down into a chair. Mr. Rite looked out at me and said, "I'll be with you two in just a minute."

I leaned over to Vinny and quietly asked, "What the heck is going on?"

He looked at me disgusted and said, "He suspended me."

My jaw dropped open. "What!".

Claire grabbed Vinny's chair and said, "Oh, I don't think so! This day ain't over."

Mr. Rite cracked his office door open and asked politely, "Mister McCleary, Miss Hanover, would you come in, please?" We both went in and sat down in that musty-smelling office, and Mr. Rite began his interrogation. "I understand you were both involved in an altercation yesterday morning? There were several witnesses and I'm trying to get to the bottom of what really happened. I've already checked both of your records and neither of you have any discrepancies with this office. Now, Mr. McCleary, why were you even involved in this matter at all?"

I couldn't believe I had to explain this to an educated person. So, I said, "Claire was in trouble. I heard her screaming so I ran to try and help her. There were no teachers or anybody helping out."

Then he really messed up, as he turned his attention to Claire. "Miss Hanover," he said in a condescending tone, "I have a witness who claims that the Garrett brothers were provoked into acting against you in the breezeway yesterday. Is there any truth to this?"

Claire snickered once before verbally clawing his eyes out. "I don't even want to know which liar told you that. Because I know it is not possible to provoke a person or persons into becoming Neanderthals and turning against a girl half their size. That is a behavior disorder or mental condition. Probably both. I also know that I was injured, my friends saved me from getting hurt worse, and you're punishing the wrong people, Mr. Rite."

I had to say something. "Excuse me, sir. Willard and Marshall Garrett were the cause of this whole thing. Why aren't they down here?"

Mr. Rite looked at the ceiling like he was annoyed and said, "This is the situation. Aside from one other witness, you three are the only ones willing to say that the Garrett boys were at the breezeway at all. And that's the witness who says they were provoked. We all must remember our places and show the proper latitude when necessary. You know, I was a science teacher long before I became principal. And it seems to me that you kids should've started learning about Newton's laws by now. I'm talking about actions and reactions and such. Does that ring any bells with you two?"

Claire cleared her throat hard and said, "Mr. Rite, I was raised to be respectful, so don't take this the wrong way. But it sounds like you may be expecting a reaction, as you put it, from old man Garrett. And maybe, just maybe, you're scared of what he'll do. Kinda like all those kids are scared to implicate his boys?"

Mr. Rite's nostrils flared as he breathed in deeply and loudly through his nose. He glared straight at Claire and said, "This office has more to deal with than you can possibly fathom, young lady."

Claire held both her blackened wrists into the air and said, "Is this the kind of latitude you're talking about? I'll have to use my wheelchair for at least a month because it hurts so badly to use my crutches. And Willard and Marshall both laughed their tails off as I tried to escape their grip.

Since we're being honest, sir, why is Vinny Deluchi being suspended?"

Mr. Rite hesitated and said, "Well, that's not your concern, but he struck another student, and suspension is automatic. Plus, Mr. Deluchi is no stranger to this office."

I couldn't let that go without sticking up for Vin. "Mr. Rite, Vinny Deluchi kept this girl from going to the hospital yesterday. It's unfair to Vinny, and it also doesn't set a very good example for everyone who saw what happened. And believe me, people saw this happen. They just don't want to say."

Mr. Rite curled his lip and said, "Remember your place, young man."

Claire had her hands in her lap and tears in her eyes. She looked like she was hurting. I know she was disappointed.

Mr. Rite got up from his big leather chair and walked around behind the two of us. "You two are something else, aren't you? Let's get you back to class, shall we? I think we can all learn something from this unfortunate event."

As we walked out of his office, Vinny was still sitting slumped over in one of those big, cushy chairs. Mr. Rite said, "Is your ride coming, son?"

Vinny grumbled, "My uncle's on his way."

We still had some time left in Ms. Meadows class and on our way back, I told Claire, "I'm getting off the bus at Vinny's house on the way home today. I gotta find out what happened in that office before we got in there."

Claire nodded in agreement. "You want me to go with you?"

"No," I said. "Thanks, but it's not necessary." I picked up a piece of gravel from the parking lot and threw it as hard and far as I could down the empty bus lane.

Skinny Vinny

I was pretty steamed all day because of the way Dudley Do Rite had done Vinny wrong. By the time school let out, my eyes were practically crossed from anger. After school, I didn't talk to anybody except Piggyback on the bus. And he had missed everything again.

He sat down with me and said, "So, Hats, you wanna fill me in on that breezeway fight? Mr. Blair held me over cause my homework was late, so I missed the entire thing. Is Claire okay?"

"Yeah, she's got bruises, but she's okay."

Piggyback leaned toward me and asked, "So was it Herschel again?"

I grimaced with disgust. "No, the coward sent his little brothers this time."

Piggyback looked worried. "Drastic! So, what are we gonna do now, Hats?"

"I'm working on it, Biggun'. I have to go talk to

Vinny right now. I'll catch you later."

As the bus pulled up close to Vinny's corner, I hopped out and started down to he and Uncle Gino's place. The new driver didn't wish me a good day or quick-draw finger guns, just stared straight ahead, chewing on a wad of gum with her mouth open. I sure missed Mr. Red.

At Vinny's, Uncle Gino answered the door and sent me to the back, where Vinny was sitting with his back to the door and headphones on his ears. I knocked but he didn't hear me. I saw some folded laundry on the bed and threw a tee shirt at him, and he turned around and laughed.

He said, "What are you doing here, Hats?"

"I gotta talk to ya, man. Is that okay?"

"Yeah, sure. Sit down." He nodded toward the couch. I scooted closer to Vinny and told him, "Vinny, I wanna know what Rite said to you today."

"No, you don't, Hats. I really don't think you want to know."

"Yes, yes, I do, please."

"All right, that butt breath told me what happened in the breezeway, only he got it all wrong. He didn't ask me. He called me a troublemaker the second I walked in that office. Hats, he had his mind made up before we ever got to the office. Just like everybody does when it concerns people like me. But it don't matter. I'm used to it."

My insides were churning like a Mississippi paddleboat. "I've got a plan and we're gonna turn this tide around. I don't have it worked out just yet. But let me think about it a little more and I'll get back with you. Trust me, okay. Things are going to get better for us. I have to get home now or my dad will have my picture on a milk carton, but I'll call you tomorrow, Vinny."

Vinny slapped my hand in appreciation and said, "Thanks for comin' by, Finn. Tell Claire I wish we'd have gotten there quicker."

I felt so bad for my friend. I forced a grin and said, "Three-day vacation isn't so bad, right? Catch ya on the flip, Vin."

The Greatest Dumb Idea Ever

I went to bed thinking about how proud I was of Claire telling Mr. Rite how the cow ate the cabbage. I mean she really handed him his shorts. I wished I was as brave as Claire.

The next morning, when I got to school, I had to pee so bad I didn't think I'd make it to the bathroom in time. I was walking as fast as I could without running in the hall and going on myself. I finally made it to the closest bathroom. Holy flood gates, what a relief.

I was rinsing my hands off at the sink and I felt a tap on the shoulder and a deep voice said, "Seems like your little sewing circle is running out of thread, Nancy pants."

I turned and was nose to chest with the king of the rattlesnakes, Herschel Garrett, blowing cigarette smoke in my face. Some kids eat Wheaties to get going in the morning. I was inhaling ash breath, first thing. Lucky me.

He thumped what was left of his smoke onto my shirt and I quickly dusted off the glowing ashes. As he started to walk out of the bathroom he looked back at me and said, "Pretty bad when the only man in your little bunch of pathetic wannabe's is a crippled girl. At least she put a knot on my stupid brother's head. What'd you do, threaten to make a speech? No wonder your mother didn't want you."

I didn't say a word. Hershel Garrett had no inkling of what he'd just done. I wasn't scared or mad or even vengeful. Because just as the cigarette smoke cleared around my head and I could see into Herschel's eyes, I heard Joshua's trumpet in my mind. And calm overtook me. It was the greatest feeling I ever had. I splashed some water on my face really fast. I had to get to class.

What a punk. With a flash of insight, I realized that the reason he always got under my skin was because I let him. That was what made me so mad. Not anymore.

Like a lifting fog, it was clear to me now. There was strength in numbers. Yes sir, strength in numbers. And I just knew I was right about this. I was done being a reject.

I knew I wasn't the only one who felt this way, either. It was time to find out just how crazy my idea was. I was excited but scared to death to know.

I thought the bus would be an ideal place to reveal the plan. It had to be in person. No phone calls, social media or second-hand information would do. I would have to make sure everybody was riding, though, which meant I had to wait until Vinny got back the day after tomorrow.

It took most of the night and most of the next day, but by the time I was through talking on the phone to everybody, I was pretty sure things were in place. But I was way too wired to sleep.

I laid in my bed and rolled this craziness over in my mind a million times, imagining how my friends were going to react. I probably slept three hours, if that, before the sun shined through the gap in my curtains, waking me before my alarm rang.

Claire was walking outside when I got to the stop. I yelled at her as I came closer, "Aren't you supposed to be using your chair for a while?"

She didn't hesitate. "Good morning to you too. Don't you have other things to attend to this morning? I feel fine, thank you."

I conceded. "Okay, Missy. Here he comes. Let's go."

Claire and I boarded the bus just like we always do and saw Mr. Red sitting behind the wheel. It was a good omen, proof that today would not be like all the million other school days.

I exchanged finger shots with Mr. Red, and then Claire gave him the biggest hug ever.

"Man, it's good to have you back," I said.

"Good to be back. Gonna be my last year, though."

"What?" Claire said. "We just got you back, and now you're going to leave again?"

"I'm gonna miss you guys, for sure," he said,

"but it's past time I retired. My wife wants me to slow down some. More likely, wants to work me half to death around the house."

He grinned, but like his heart wasn't in it.

"I'm not going to think about that," Claire said, echoing my feelings a hundred percent. "We're just glad to have you back." As Claire pulled herself up and turned the corner away from Mr. Red's seat, I glanced back as the door closed behind me. The gust of wind nearly blew my hat off. But I caught it and shoved it back onto my head.

I realized I was moving slowly on purpose because I was so nervous about this. Yesterday I was excited but now that it was time I didn't know if I could go through with it.

As I was making my way back to sit down, I was trying to see who all was already on the bus. As I scanned the rows, I had nearly convinced myself that this wasn't the right day to do it. Funny how yesterday I was all gung ho and now I felt like a scared little rabbit.

I wasn't paying much attention to where I was

stepping exactly, and I stumbled a little bit on a backpack that was sticking out in the aisle and I bumped into Ethan Matthews' leg. He is just about the smallest kid in the whole school. I said, "Oh man, I'm sorry, Ethan. I didn't see that backpack. Are you okay?" He shrugged. "I'm not hurt. I saw it coming. Don't worry about it."

Then I realized what I had just said. Ethan. Like my dad's friend. I said to myself, Oh, I got this.

I don't really believe in fate or Karma, but I wasn't crazy enough to ignore a reminder like that. Everyone was on the bus except Tommy and Piggyback. And we were just about to pick them up.

We were all kind of sitting in a cluster when we got to Piggyback's stop, nobody saying much yet, so it was sort of quiet on the bus. Well, until he boarded.

Piggyback jumped on the bus wound up like a three-day clock. He grabbed the silver pole at the front of the bus, swung around it and yelled to everyone, "Good morning, campers! Why so quiet? Are we going to a funeral or a library opening?"

As he made his way toward the back of the bus, he just kept talking. "Watch yourself, the aisle killer's comin' through. Okay, Hats, lay it on us. What's up your sleeve, brotherman?"

I had to tell him, "Tommy's not here yet. Just a couple more minutes, Piggyback."

Piggyback grumbled to himself but said, "Are you sure Daddy Long Legs is riding the bus today?"

"Yes, Piggyback," I said. "Just look out the window." There was Tommy, waiting at his stop. "Now, would you cool it, please?"

"Cool as a pig in mud, Bubba," Piggyback insisted.

Tommy got on the bus and headed straight back to sit near me and Claire. Tommy is so tall his cowlick practically scrapes the top of the bus.

"Mornin', everybody," he said, yawning. "Are we all here?"

I counted them off in my head. "Yep, I believe this is everybody. Y'all scrunch in so I don't have to talk loud." Everybody was sitting within a seat or two apart, so they could hear me pretty well without everybody else on the bus butting into our business.

"I don't have to tell you guys that we all have a lot in common. That's what brought us together as friends a long time ago. But some of the things that set us apart as individuals also make us targets for persecution." I'd practiced that line all night and was proud of myself for thinking of it. I sounded almost like Claire. "You all know what I'm talking about. Well, every one of us has taken heat in some way from the creep patrol in this town just because we're different. I'm sick of it."

Piggyback interrupted and said, "Dude, the Gettysburg address wasn't this long. You gonna make a point?"

Vinny chimed in from over my shoulder saying, "Let him talk, Piggyback."

Piggyback was right, though. I was beating around the bush. I got my mind right and just talked straight.

"Okay, here it is. I'm through being pushed

around by the Trackers in this town. I'm tired of being called rejects. I wanna form a club and call ourselves the Differents. My dad says if you don't stand up for yourself, you never amount to anything. I believe it. I also believe in you guys. And I always will. Now, you can think it over, but if you're with me on this, our first club meeting will be held today after school at the old baseball field on Red-stitch Road, home plate, rain or shine."

You could have heard a pin drop in our little section. I didn't expect to receive a collective cheer, but I also didn't expect crickets. But that's pretty much what I got except for Vinny. He was sitting in the seat behind me and after everybody kind of started talking about other stuff again, he leaned up close to my ear and said to me, "Hats, I don't need all day. I'll be there. I'm in a hundred percent, man."

We Don't Do Rainouts

I reached back with my hand over my shoulder and grabbed Vinny's hand as tightly as I could squeeze it. That meant so much. Even if he was the only one to go along with this crazy idea, it was huge to me.

I was a nervous wreck all day. Nobody wanted to really talk about what they had decided—or hadn't for that matter.

I asked Piggyback at lunch and he said, "I don't know, Hats, sounds like we might have a bigger target on our backs with this club?"

Claire was quiet in Ms. Meadows class, but she finally told me that she was with me when we got to Math.

It looked like I'd be sweating bullets about Tommy and Piggyback all the way to the ball field. Some motivator I was turning out to be. By the time the last bell rang, I felt like a complete fool for thinking I could change anything.

"Okay, God," I said aloud as I left the school grounds that afternoon. "I'd be grateful if you'd give my friends a little nudge."

I decided to walk over to Asa's Junkyard. It was only a block away from school. Asa lets me keep my old bike in one of his sheds for when I don't have a ride home. Asa Baines is a hero to me. He's the only guy in our town that ever played major league baseball. Asa played two seasons for the Kansas City Royals. And while that's not a long time, he did play in their minor league farm system for many years. I had been taking instruction from him since I started little league. He and my Dad go way back. Today I planned on riding my bike over to Red-Stitch. I was taking my time because I wanted to give any others, if there were any, time to get down there first.

I rode my bike about halfway to the ballpark and it started to sprinkle a little bit. I just knew that would be enough to ruin things. Just my stinking luck, on top of an unlikely situation, I get bad weather setting in.

By the time I got to Red-Stitch Road, my hat needed a windshield wiper. Nobody in their right mind was coming out in this mess. At the top of the hill, I dropped my old bike to the ground. I was still a little way from the field and I couldn't tell if anybody was down there. You had to jump an old gate to get to the field because it had been rusted shut forever, and there was a grove of tallow trees where the bleachers used to be. I couldn't see through those stupid trees to the field.

I did see one thing before I jumped that rusty old gate, though, and it made my heart ping. Piggyback Kidd's bicycle was lying on the ground just down from mine. I couldn't believe it. I guess God had been listening. I looked to the heavens and mouthed silent thanks.

I took off running for the field as fast as I could. As I rounded those trees and made it within sight of the old diamond, there they all were in the pouring rain, like a pack of loyal, wet dogs. Every one of them gathered around home plate, just waiting for me.

"We didn't think you'd ever get here, Hats," Piggyback hollered with his giant cheeks pressed against the backstop fencing.

Claire, of all people, was standing propped on those crutches, in the on-deck circle. She did have enough sense to be wearing a yellow slicker. She kept it in her locker. I quickly made my way down to join everybody on the field. Then Claire asked, "So, what's the plan, Hats?"

"Well", I said loudly over the sound of the downpour. It's simple. We meet regularly so we know who's having trouble with who. We communicate at school about any problems. We stick together and stand up for one another. I believe a bully hates to be called out. And I'm not talking about fighting. We have to outsmart them. I also believe once the Trackers find out we've banded together, they're going to be jealous."

Vinny asked in a serious tone, "Hats, you can't

be serious about that part?"

I looked Vinny straight in the eyes. "I know it, Vin. If there's one thing I've learned from all those old movies I watched with my dad, it's that even the hardest of hearts wanna to be on the right side of things."

He looked like I'd grown a second head. I guess it did sound a little sappy, but I liked the sound of what I'd said.

I couldn't get over these guys being here. I said, "By the way, did any of you nuts notice that it's about to come a freakin' flood out here?"

Piggyback thundered back, "You said rain or shine, didn't you? What makes you think we don't listen to you?"

"You're right. That's what I said."

We'd all taken shelter in one of the dugouts since the rain wasn't letting up. However, that old dugout wasn't exactly watertight anymore. And man was it loud on that leaky tin roof. Sounded like fireworks or an old shoot 'em up movie. But it was way better than home plate.

Claire looked at me and grinned so big. "I love this so much. I'm really proud of you, Finn McCleary."

And even Tommy added his two cents, "It's about time we stood up for ourselves and did something."

Piggyback stood up and picked me up by the waist. "This is way drastic, dude! Sorry I was so slow to the party."

I found enough presence of mind to say, "Put me down, Piggyback. I appreciate it. But listen, before y'all get carried away. This is not about me. It's about us. It's about what we represent. And anybody who understands that should be welcome to join. From now on, we are the Differents."

"That's us!" Vinny yelled. "Yeah, you're right." Tommy shouted back. Everybody was very excited.

It was an amazing thing to see. And I wasn't about to ruin it by running my mouth anymore. We celebrated the fact that we were different, and we were okay with it. And we sure didn't care who knew it. We enjoyed every wet minute of it.

141

Ms. Meadows Collects Donations

Claire called me a couple of hours after school and asked if I could come over just for a few minutes. She said she had something for me to bring to Ms. Meadows. She didn't want to explain on the phone, so I didn't press the matter. I just asked my dad if I could go and I went.

Claire only lives about a mile from me and my Dad so it's no big deal for me to ride my bike there. When I got to Claire's door, I could tell right away that she didn't feel well.

I said, "You're sick, huh?"

She rolled her eyes and said, "I have a little fever so my mom's keeping me home tomorrow." We walked into the house, sat down, and she continued. "That's why I asked you to come over. Ms. Meadows is collecting for the winter drive tomorrow. I have a coat I think will fit Grace perfectly. Will you please give it to Ms. Meadows for me and tell her who it's for?"

I looked at Claire a little sideways. "Okay, but who the heck is Grace?"

"Finn McCleary, I swear. Can't you remember anything? Eugenia! Grace is her middle name. Remember now?"

"Oh yeah, okay. Geez Louise, Claire! Don't get your fever in an uproar. I'll handle it."

Claire gave me a concerned look. "Are you sure?"

"I promise." I tried to reassure her, touching the side of her arm.

"Thank you, Hats. She never has a jacket when it's cold. My mom bought the coat for herself, but she was allergic to the down on the collar. It's practically new," she added, proudly. I took the box with the coat in it under my arm, told Claire to get to feeling better and took off for home on my bike.

As the wind blew in my face on my way home, I worried about Claire. Every year about this time, she starts to have difficulties with her condition.

I don't know how many times she's wound up in the hospital having to get treatments for her bones. She really hates it and I hate it for her.

The doctors told her a couple of years ago it would be a lot easier on her if she stopped walking altogether. They said her bones had lost the strength to support her weight, and walking was too rigorous for her. Her bones had become brittle. But you might as well tell Claire to stop breathing.

Just like tonight, Claire dismisses ever being less than a hundred percent. Me, on the other hand, I'm ready to recruit pall bearers every time I get the flu.

For the past several years, Mrs. Angelo had overseen a program that helped provide winter jackets and coats for students who were less fortunate than most. This year would be the first that Ms. Meadows would oversee that project.

There had been flyers all over school for this thing for weeks and weeks. Personally, I was glad it was finally going to come and go. I was sick of pastel-colored copy paper taped up everywhere you looked. The whole school looked like a fourth-grade slumber party.

We were about five weeks away from our cold weather. And even though we don't have extreme winters, without a coat of some kind, it can be uncomfortable, and lots of kids get sick.

My plan was to try to make it to Ms. Meadows class a couple of minutes early to tell her about Claire's coat. And I had to make sure Eugenia was nowhere around when I did. I was the first to admit that I was a terrible whisperer. My voice has this horrible tendency to carry like an echo in a canyon. But I was going to be very careful today. As bad as I would feel if Eugenia didn't get the coat because of me, a winter's cold wouldn't hold a candle to the wrath of Claire Hanover on my poor soul if I were to screw this up.

Much to my own surprise, I managed to reach Ms. Meadows classroom about the same time she did. She had just gone into the room as I reached the door. No one else had made it there yet. I hurried in to get this over with. She was already fussing with papers at her desk.

I went straight over and said, "Good morning, Ms. Meadows. Can I talk to you a second?"

She looked up over her glasses and said, "Good morning, Finn. What is it?"

"Um, I have a donation from Claire. She's sick today. She wanted…"

She stopped me right in my tracks and said, "We're doing that at the end of class. Just put the box on that table right over there. Thank you very much."

What a great start. I had it planned perfectly too. Now I had to try to tell her with everybody around. I'm not a freaking magician. If the guys saw me whispering to the teacher, I'd never hear the end of it.

When Piggyback got to class, he was all concerned about our English assignment. He kept hounding me, asking over and over, "Did you finish the whole thing, Hats? Can you show me the last two sections?

I don't get that part."

I told him, "Pigster, English isn't until sixth period. That's after lunch. We'll get you straight before class, honest. But I need you to help me with a situation before then."

Piggyback, sounding satisfied, agreed. "Okay, Hats, what is it?"

"Claire's sick today. I gotta give Ms. Meadows a donation from her that's intended for Eugenia. I need you to distract Eugenia toward the end of class when I go up to talk to the teacher."

Piggyback grinned from ear to ear and said, "Piece of cake, old buddy. Distraction is my main attraction. That's right up my alley."

Ms. Meadows ended up saving about fifteen minutes at the end of class to handle the donations. She stood in front of her desk and said to us all, "Everyone, there's only a few minutes remaining today. Let's use this time to collect for the winter donations. If you haven't already put what you've brought on the side table, you may do so now."

Several people got up to do just as Ms. Meadows instructed. Then she decided to talk some more. "All right students, I'm going to begin an inventory of these items and I'll allow you some free time if you can keep the noise to a minimum."

I looked at Piggyback and motioned my head toward Eugenia. He gave me a thumbs-up and headed back toward her desk. When I saw Piggyback starting a conversation with Eugenia, that was my cue to make my move to speak with Ms. Meadows. She had taken a seat at the table on the side of the room where all the donations were stacked. I went over and sat in another chair near her.

I said to her very softly, "Ms. Meadows, I have to talk to you." Again, she looked at me over her glasses but this time she said, "Okay, Finn."

Relieved, I glanced toward the far side of the room. From the corner of my eye, I could see Piggyback gaining comedic strength. His arms were flailing, with pencils as walrus' tusks hanging from his mouth.

I said, "I have to tell you about the box I

brought in this morning. It wasn't from me. It was from Claire Hanover. She's sick today. But she asked me to bring it and she really wants you to try and get this coat to Eugenia Rojas. It's super important to Claire. It's a good coat and Eugenia, well actually she prefers to be called Grace—it's what her Mom calls her, I think—but anyhow, Ms. Meadows, she can't know we gave it to her, okay? It's the dark brown box. Thank you very much."

She put her hand on my shoulder and took her glasses off. Then she said to me, "Thank you, Finn. And you tell Claire I'll take care of this for her. I'm making a note of it right now, so I don't forget. And tell her to get well quickly and hurry back to class." I nodded and turned to go, but her hand on my shoulder stopped me. "What you and Vinny did for Claire. . .That was very brave of you."

I shrugged. It wasn't brave. It was the only thing we could have done.

She went on. "I've been thinking about respect, and I've decided. . .well. . .I suppose there's no real harm in letting you wear the hat."

I felt a flood of relief. Even though I'd gotten by without it, it would feel great to put it on. "Thanks, Ms. Meadows. Oh, and one more thing." She lifted her eyebrows and I rushed on. "My name. It isn't Finn. I mean, it is, but it's not. Everybody calls me Hats."

"Hats," she said, and glanced at the clock. It was almost time for the bell to ring. "See you in class tomorrow, Hats."

As I walked back to my desk, I looked toward the back of the class and Eugenia Grace was laughing hysterically at that big electrical storm we all call Piggyback Kidd, coming through in the clutch.

The Hospital

The next few days were not good for any of us. The Garretts had ramped up their hatefulness, and despite Claire's hard-headed refusal to admit she was sick, her fever didn't seem to want to break. Her mom took her to the doctor and Claire texted me on their way home.

I had gotten home from school already and was planning to call her, so when her name popped up on my phone screen, I got really glad.

I couldn't wait to hear her news. I quickly read what she had written.

"Well, they're putting me in jail again." It said. "I've gotta get another round of those stupid calcium injections. And they say I have to be on monitors for at least three days in the hospital. Whoop whoop. So, how's it going with you, Finn?"

I replied saying, "Forget about me. I'm fine. Listen, I know you hate this. But it's only a few days and it'll be over. We're all behind you a thousand percent. I'll be up to see you tomorrow after school."

She texted back again. "Can you tell the gang what's going on for me? I'm kind of tired, Hats. We're just running home to pack a bag and heading to the hospital tonight."

And I just assured her, "Don't you worry about a thing, Sweet Face." You just do what the doctors say and get some rest."

That night, I let everybody know about Claire's situation. The next day, when I got home, I told my dad about Claire and asked if he could drop me off at the hospital, so I could visit her for a while? He told me we could go right after dinner.

There's a bookstore right across the street from the hospital and my Dad could live there, I think. He said he'd wait for me there while I saw Claire. When I got off the elevator on Claire's floor, I saw her Mom getting on another elevator. I don't think she saw me.

Her room wasn't that far from the nurse's station. I went right through the open door to find her dozing off to sleep. I didn't want to freak her out, so I sat down lightly beside her on the bed and she opened her big brown eyes and smiled.

"Hey," she said happily. "How long have you been here?"

I touched her hand and told her, "Only a minute or two. How ya feelin'?"

"Good right now, fever's down. No shots yet."

"You're gonna be fine, I know it. I want you to know that Ms. Meadows did what you asked with the coat. Grace has it now."

Claire smiled sweetly and said, "Oh, good. I'm glad to hear that. Thank you, Finn." Claire propped herself up in the bed and took her hairbrush from the side table and quickly straightened her hair. "Oh, Piggyback and Vinny came up earlier. Thanks for telling them I was here."

I looked over at the small bed in the next curtain a few feet from Claire's bed. "Is that where your Mom is gonna sleep?"

She leaned up and looked over. "Yep, she went

down to eat supper."

"That's what I figured. I saw her getting on the elevator. You mind if I check it out?"

Claire turned her palms up, shrugged, and said "Go ahead." I ducked behind the curtain and plopped down on that bed like I was a patient. Claire couldn't even see me because I left the curtain closed.

Just as I about to pretend to ring for a sponge bath, I heard someone else come into the room. So, I stayed put. I heard the nurse say, "Just a few minutes, it's almost time to change her IV."

When the visitor said, "I won't take long," I knew it was Eugenia. I had to hear this. The curtain wasn't lined up right for me to see her, so I was just praying she would talk loud enough for me to hear this. She must have had on those thirty-seven-pound combat boots she usually wore because I could hear her walk up to the bed loud and clear.

Claire spoke first saying, "Grace, I'm surprised to see you. How did you know I was here?"

Sounding rather awkward, Eugenia said, "Claire, I'm sorry you're sick. Some kids were saying at school you were in the hospital. Plus, I wanted to show you that I found this." I crawled to the very top of that cot and just barely peeked around the corner of the curtain to try and see what in the world she was talking about. Eugenia had her arm stretched out in front of her with a crumpled piece of paper in her hand.

Claire looked confused. "What is it?"

Pushing it at her, Eugenia said, "Take it." Then, without hesitation, Eugenia turned and walked straight out of the hospital room.

Claire took the paper and held it in front of her and said out loud, "This is my mother's bank slip."

I opened the curtain and Claire looked at me and sighed. "Hats, I think I've made a terrible mistake. I should have known she'd find out who gave her that coat."

"I don't know why that should matter. She needed a coat, you gave her one, end of story."

"Oh, Hats." She gave me one of her long looks. "We were just starting to be friends, and then I went and hurt her pride. I hope she'll forgive me."

I was still trying to wrap my head around the idea of being friends with Eugenia. Then a thought occurred to me. "I think she already has," I said. At Claire's puzzled look, I pointed to the bank slip in her hand. "She left you that. But she kept the coat."

I went over to sit in the chair beside her bed. And just as we were about to discuss this, the nurse came in and changed the IV and checked Claire's vital signs. I moved again and sat in the big chair across from the bed until they were done.

About fifteen minutes later, the nurse had finally gone, and her hospital phone rang.

Claire answered, and turned on her side. She only talked for a minute and it was practically a mumble. I didn't hear a word. When she got off the phone she told me, "That was Grace on the phone. I told her it only made sense for the coat to go to a friend instead of a stranger, but then she got cut off in mid-sentence. I guess her phone died."

I said, "Claire, you do remember that you're sick, right?"

She rolled her eyes at me. "I'm not dying, for crying out loud."

My stomach gave a lurch. Somehow saying she wasn't made me worry that she might. While I was trying to figure out what to say, Mrs. Hanover returned from the cafeteria and rescued me from the conversation. She was always so nice to me. She hugged me and said, "How are you, Cutie pie?"

"I'm fine, Mrs. H. How about you?"

She stepped over to Claire's bed and brushed her hair away from her face with her hand. "We're both pretty exhausted, Finn. We just need to get our girl through these treatments and get back home. Did they bring your dinner yet, baby?"

Claire sank down into her pillow and said, "No ma'am. Not yet. Grace Rojas just left."

By then, I just felt useless. "Well. If there's

anything you guys need, just let me know and I'll bring it to you. I'm sure my dad's probably read half the books across the street by now. I better go. Claire, you know I'm thinking about you all the time. Praying for you too. I'll call tomorrow, okay?"

I ran over and kissed her hand. She grabbed my hand, looked up at me with those big doe eyes, and said, "Thank your Daddy for bringing you and staying all this time, you hear me? Goodnight, Finn."

Mrs. Hanover echoed the sentiment, "Thank you for coming Finn. Goodnight."

As I cornered passed the bathroom and moved toward the door leaving Claire's room, I heard Claire's mom say, "He's a fine boy."

"I know, Momma," Claire said softly.

I guess they thought I had already left. I squeezed sideways through the partly opened door. I hated to leave Claire in that place, but I felt a little taller all the way to the bookstore.

The Challenge

Everybody was pretty bummed out about Claire being in the hospital, so the next afternoon, we decided to walk over to Clark's after school to get a drink and hang out for a while. We had all been going to Mr. and Mrs. Clark's little grocery to get cold drinks for as long as I could remember.

They had one of those old timey kinds of chest coolers and you couldn't even see your hand for the smoke when you reached in to get your drink, it was so cold. Plus, they had every flavor in the world. Strawberry, orange crush, nugrape, cream soda, root beer, and all the regular stuff too. And they were the nicest people in the world.

After we finished our drinks, we headed slowly homeward. As usual, Piggyback had managed to end up wearing half of his strawberry soda. That's probably because one was never enough for him, and he downed them like we were crossing the Sahara Desert.

We walked for two blocks or so and we weren't far from the railroad tracks. I looked down a cross street and heading in our direction were the Garrett boys. I wasn't the only one that spotted them either.

"Act normal, maybe they didn't see us," Piggyback said, nervously.

Vinny, leading with his chin up, got in front of us a little and said confidently, "Relax, they don't own the road. Just keep moving like we're moving." And that's just what we did. But so did the Trackers, and they were closing in fast.

Herschel and his brothers ran toward us, and that's when it started to hit the fan. Rocks flew in and landed right in front of us. Then one hit Vinny in the back. Another hit me just above the left kidney. It hurt like heck. We started moving faster as the rocks came in quicker and harder. Beside me, Piggyback was breathing hard. The back of my neck felt hot. We'd turned the other cheek until we'd flat run out of cheeks.

Vinny's fists were both fully clenched now, and

he stopped dead in the middle of the road. We all stopped. Vinny turned around and Herschel was twenty feet away. Herschel reared back and threw another piece of gravel. It hit Piggyback right in the face.

Vinny started toward the Garretts, fuming.

I knew how mad he was, but I couldn't let him fight again. I stepped in front of Vinny and said, "What the heck do you want, Herschel?"

Herschel kicked rocks in my direction. "You panty waists are stinking up our road. You just don't learn, do you?"

I was so over being scared of this meathead. "Look Herschel, I know you got about as much restraint as a team of donkeys, but you know as well we do that this road connects the school to all our houses. So, unless you got a helicopter we can borrow, you need to crawl back in your cave."

Mastermind number two, Willard, decided to chime in. "Hey Blubber-Butt," he called to Piggyback. "Did you eat a live dog on the way over here? Looks like it bled all over your shirt."

"It's strawberry, Willard," Piggyback barked back, as he held his scratched cheek.

Marshall looked over at Piggyback and said, "I think I'll go get my gun and chase you down like a wild hog. Then maybe you'll learn your lesson."

Herschel picked up another rock to throw in my direction and asked, "Why can't you retards just ride your little short bus and stay off our road altogether?"

I stepped to the side and caught the rock. It stung my palm, but I was too mad to care. I slammed it down as hard as I could. "Hey," I yelled over to Herschel, who was whispering something to Willard. "Hey, Herschel, can you listen for a second? Marshall just gave me a great idea and I think you're gonna like it."

Marshall threw a rock right at my feet and hollered, "Shut your pie hole, Red."

Herschel gave him a stern look. "Be quiet, Marshall. I wanna hear this great idea. Let me hear it, Mcphead."

"All right. If you Garretts really think you're so much better than Piggyback Kidd here, I have a challenge for you. I say the Kidd can take all of you, with his fat self, in a race, say of a hundred yards."

Herschel looked at me like I'd handed him a bag full of money. Then he snickered and said, "Get real, dude."

"I'm dead serious." I stepped closer to him. "Listen to me. We can use the school track. We'll even sell tickets. The Kidd has to outrun all three of you and your cousin Hermann to be the winner. Only one of you guys have to cross the finish line before Piggyback.

"If you guys win, you keep the ticket money and the Kidd wears a tee shirt with *Look at Me* on the front and *I'm Really Fat* on the back to school. If the Kidd wins, y'all agree to stop harassing him completely and you carry his books to class for three days straight. Plus, the money goes to us."

Herschel rubbed his head and kicked the ground a couple of times. Finally, he said, "You talk a lot, McWeirdo. There's no way in the world that fatso could outrun a fencepost, much less take a Garrett."

Piggyback came up behind me and said, breathing in my ear, "This is a really bad time to lose your mind entirely. Seriously bad timing."

When no one had said a thing for a minute, Herschel proclaimed loudly, "It's a deal. Two weeks from Saturday. Two o'clock. Set it up. I guess you girls are used to being humiliated."

"Great," I said, feeling relieved. "See you guys at the finish line. Let's go home, boys." We all ran for about fifty yards to get some distance between us and the tension of that situation. When we slowed down and began to try to breathe again, I started to catch it good.

Vinny said, "Are you crazy or something? Hats, how on God's green earth is Piggyback going to outrun those man children?"

Before I could even begin to answer, Piggyback started in again. "Why do you hate me, suddenly? This is the most hair-brained idea ever."

I sighed deeply and said, "We're going to win. Just wait, boys. Trust me on this, Piggyback. All those midget brains are gonna hear in two weeks is the thunder of your giant hamhocks quaking the earth in front of them."

Junkyard Pig

We decided to go back to my house and discuss how we were going to pull off this unlikely victory. I have an old treehouse that we all barely fit into anymore, but we climbed up and squeezed in anyway.

"Okay, guys, listen," I said, when we were all settled. "Do I need to remind you how Piggyback got his nickname?"

Vinny leaned in and said, "Everybody knows, Hats."

I said, "So any argument that he has the strongest legs in school?"

Tommy shrugged. "None here."

"Personally," I added, "I don't know anyone with more determination except Claire, and she can't run. So... We have two weeks to train and get you mentally ready to do something great, Piggyback. I know you can do this if you decide you can. But you have to want it. You can be sure the Garretts are gonna spend the next two weeks coming up with dirty tricks instead of training. So, there's our first advantage.

Vinny scooted over close to the Kidd and said, "Imagine how freakin' great it's gonna feel to beat those turds. How many times have they laughed in your face? You gotta do this, Georgie! There just ain't two ways about it. We're gonna get you ready. Ready as a rock, boy. But you're doin' this, big man. Are you hearing me?"

Piggyback slapped both his big legs and stood up, hitting his head on a rafter. "Ow! That's a great start. Okay, but I'm going to need you guys' help. Let's beat the snot out of those morons."

We all hurrahed Piggyback on, patting him on the back and encouraging him to win. And then I shared my idea about getting ready for the race.

"Guys, I have an idea about training. I'm going to call Asa Baines tonight to see if he'll let us use the junkyard after school to train Piggyback."

Piggyback didn't like the idea at all. "Hats, you want me to work out at the junkyard? Seriously?"

I shrugged. "Well, yeah. It's close to school, plus we can set up a cool obstacle course to work on your balance and stuff. Not to mention the pointers that Asa could give us. Does anyone have a better place in mind? I'm open to suggestions."

Piggyback started laughing like he knew something we didn't and said, "All right, talk to Asa."

Asa Baines was one of my favorite people in our sleepy little town. He had run the junkyard ever since he quit minor league baseball. And that was a very long time ago.

Now Asa was a lot older, but he had some of the best stories. I thought they were great stories, anyway, but then I love anything about baseball. Lately I'd had trouble concentrating on my other hobbies like reading and drawing—thoughts of my Mom and of Herschel Garrett kept getting in the way—but I thanked God regularly for keeping me interested in baseball.

Asa had lived things I could only dream of. I called him about using the junkyard for our workouts and as I suspected he said come on. I let the guys know the next day that training was a go, and we decided to head over Saturday morning to check out the junkyard together.

Asa was probably the biggest man in town. He looked like a walking Sequoia. He no longer had any hair on his head and his skin was the color of a freshly varnished bedpost. I don't know if that was natural or was from being in the sun all the time.

When we got inside the fence at the yard, Asa came around the corner from his office to meet us. I ran out in front to shake his hand and thank him for allowing us to use the junkyard.

We all gathered around the big man and he said in a booming voice, "Hello boys. Who's our racer?"

Piggyback jerked his hand firmly into the air and said, "I am, Mr. Asa."

"Well," Mr. Asa said, nodding toward me, "I told Shortstop here that I would help you fellas get started. But then you're on your own because I stay pretty busy around here. Step on up here, doughboy. Stand here right in front of me. Say, you're G. H's boy, aren't you?"

Piggyback swallowed hard and said, "Yes sir."

"Now, tell me, can you see the top of my head, young man?"

Piggyback stepped back and leaned his head back as far as he could, his eyes strained toward the peak of this mountainous man. "No sir, he said. I can't see the top of your head. You're too tall."

Asa cleared his throat sounding like what I thought Zeus might sound like, and said, "How old are you, boy?"

Piggyback cocked his head. "I'll be thirteen in two months."

"I'm gonna tell you something, young'un'. When I was thirteen I looked just like you. A heavy-set doughboy. See how big your durn feet are? You're gonna be just as big as me someday. It won't be long, big man, all these boys will be looking up to you, just like you're looking up to me right now. I know you don't believe it. But it's true."

Asa turned toward me and pointed toward his office,

saying, "Shortstop, go to my office and get the orange vest on my desk and bring it out here, won't ya please?" I brought the vest back, completely confused about what it was for.

Asa handed the vest to Piggyback. "Okay. Put this vest on, George. Now the plan is for you to wear this the whole time you're in the yard. It has pockets on the inside and we're going to put weights in them. You'll get used to working out with the added weight and by the time the race gets here you'll feel light as a feather without it."

He turned to me. "Shortstop, you and Vinny grab that box of magnets on the red table in stall three and carry them over here. Be careful, they're heavy."

He wasn't lying. It took both of us to carry it back. They were very heavy and full of round magnets that Asa started stuffing into the vest. He got about three of them in before Piggyback started complaining about the weight.

Once that was done, we had Piggyback do some

lunges with the vest and a couple of sprints. By then, he was bent over clenching his kneecaps and breathing like a jackass sounds.

I didn't want to cripple him during the first workout, so I came to Piggyback's rescue and told Asa we had to get home.

We all thanked Asa for his help and headed toward the gate. Piggyback was sweating bullets and as he wiped the sweat from his face, he asked, "Can somebody help me off with this mafia fishing jacket, please?"

I took one side and Tommy took the other and we peeled the weighted vest off our drenched, very tired friend. "It was a great start, big guy," I said. "You're gonna be sore, though. Soak your bones tonight."

Piggyback said, "Let's get out of here. I'm ready for bed."

After Piggyback had slumped down the gravel road a little way, I whispered to the guys, "On three, everybody yell, Get some sleep, champ!"

So, in unison, we all yelled it as loud as we could. He had turned the corner on the curvy drive, out of our sight. But he wasn't so far down the road that we couldn't hear that distinctive belly laugh of his reverberate off the pine trees.

Old Thirty-Eight

I told my dad I would go to the evening service at church so that I could skip morning church. Vinny and I wanted to get an early start setting up the obstacle course for Piggyback at the junkyard.

We found a good spot away from the main junk where there was some soft grass and only a few old cars. We used some tires and beat up orange cones and spread them out in between the cars for Piggyback to run in between and around.

As well as Piggyback had been doing with his training, every now and then he would just crash and burn. And like any good Pig, he'd end up face first in the dirt. We had to make sure that where he was training was clear of any debris that he might land on and become injured. That meant our job involved more planning than we anticipated in the beginning.

After we were done, we decided to get cleaned up and go see Claire at the hospital. I had already

broken one phone screen a while back when the guys
and I were horsing around so I didn't bring my
cell with me to the junkyard. I gave her a quick
call from Mr. Asa's phone, and she told me they
were signing discharge papers at that very moment.
She'd be home in two hours and would call me then.
I let her know we had a lot to talk about.

I gave Vinny the good news and went home to wait
for Claire's call. After she said she'd be back at
school the next day, I told her the whole Herschel
saga and how the race came about. She volunteered
to make tickets to sell for the race, and I hung up
grinning and shaking my head. That Claire. Nothing
could keep her down.

Asa kept promising us that, if we kept training
hard, he'd show us this mystery car he'd been
working on forever. He kept it covered under a
big tarp in the back of his shop area. He had our
curiosity up, but every day he put us off again.
He told us it was a nineteen thirty-eight Buick
Y, whatever that is. So, in my mind, it was a
lawnmower with doors. I mean, do the math. This
thing was older than my dad. But this tarp was

enormous. It just didn't make sense to me.

Thursday before the race rolled around, and we were back among the junk for Piggyback's last workout. Everybody agreed that he needed and deserved to rest on Friday before the race. None of us could believe how much weight Piggyback had shed. The junkyard was saturated in his sweat. We started calling it Sweat Hog Lake. We had all started huddling together before he began his workout every day.

This time, as we huddled up, we heard a yell, "Hey knot heads! Hang on a minute." And coming through the gate, ninety to nothing, was Claire, propped up high in her power chair, cruising straight toward us. "I decided to crash your party, Piggyback."

Piggyback stepped toward her and said, "Hey Sweet Face, I'm glad to see you." She leaned forward to hug Piggyback and abruptly pulled back, saying, "Ick, Piggyback. You smell!"

From the office, Asa hollered out, "You fellas want to see her now? C'mon!" Without even thinking, everybody bolted toward the shop. I jumped on the back of Claire's chair, balancing on her tip bars and told her to follow the boys.

She frowned, hands on the controls of her chair. "Where are we going?"

"Just go!" I said. You're gonna love this."

We got to the carport where the big surprise was waiting. Asa came around the side of the building with keys in his hand and said, "Now, I told you this car is very old. And I'm not done with her. Matter of fact, the tires aren't even on her right now. But I got her running. So, let me pull the veil off and see what you think."

Asa reached way under the front of the car, pulled the tarp loose, and jerked the whole thing forward. It slid off in slow motion, like a giant handkerchief. Underneath was this black tank in a tuxedo. This massively sleek convertible machine was unlike anything we had ever seen.

Asa opened the door, sat down in the driver's seat and cranked the engine. We all jumped back when it started. It didn't sound like a car. It roared, but it was more a feeling than a sound. I looked down at my shoes and my shoelaces were bouncing off the tops of my shoes from the vibration. This thing was more like an airplane. The Bat Mobile had nothing on this ride. Asa revved the engine a couple of times and the hairs on my arms tingled. He let it idle for a bit. Then he killed it.

We all said, "Aw, man!" at the same time. I said, "Crank it up again, Asa!"

"Naw, that's enough for today," he said firmly, and yanked the tarp back over the car. "Well, there it is, guys. That's my baby. When your race is all said and done, I'll take you all for a ride if I can get her street legal again."

The past two weeks Piggyback Kidd had spent as much time in that old grimy junkyard after school as Asa's prized Thirty-eight Buick. If anybody deserved a ride in that car, it was the Big Guy.

About Mom

My mind had been tied up like a wet shoelace for so long that it was getting harder and harder to clearly remember my mother. The image of Hannah kept getting mixed up with my old memories. What I did remember, though, was the way she made me feel when I was doubting myself. I had decided I was going to call her. I just wanted to hear her voice again. I had wasted so much time being selfish.

My dad had made no secret that he kept in touch with her.

I wasn't going to use my cell because she wouldn't recognize the number and may not answer. I decided to use the extension in the den. Just as I finished dialing her number, my dad walked in the room. I quickly planted the receiver back on its cradle.

"Hiya Bud. Who you talking to?"

"Nobody," I said nervously. "I tried to get Claire, but I got her voicemail."

"Well, that works out because I'd like to talk to you for a bit. You up to it?"

"Oh Dad, what about? Not a lecture tonight, please."

"No, nothing like that. Come sit down." He sat down on the couch and patted the cushion beside him. "I want to tell you a story about something I think you've forgotten. It's about your Mom."

"Dad, I really don't think I need to—"

He just patted the cushion again until I sighed and plopped down beside him. "I'll tell you the reason I bring it up. It's because I've noticed you've stopped doing some of the things you used to enjoy, like reading those mystery books and sketching pictures. Your mother was always better than I was at keeping track of you.

"Anyway, I know you still miss her. I do too. I feel like I need to tell you a couple of things. When you were little, you meant more to her than me or anything. Now I know someone your age would rather eat dirt than hear adults talk about feelings. So, I'm gonna try not to make you vomit. But it's important for you to understand your mom's real attitude toward you and your sister, especially the way things turned out for us.

"She used to sit with you in her lap and run her fingers through your red hair and she would just carry on about how lucky she was to have such a unique and wonderful child. And if anybody ever made fun of you, your mother was ready to defend you tooth and nail."

My dad looked me dead in the eye with his hand on my shoulder as he reminded me all about my mother. I didn't need trips down memory lane at this point but somehow what my dad was saying touched me as soft and cool as the other side of the pillow. I didn't protest as he went on.

"I guess all mothers love their children to some degree, Finn, but your mother had a big love for both her children. I'd be surprised if you don't remember that story she used to tell you about the little Irish boy born with hair black as coal. And how he climbed the parish ladder to pray for red hair like his brothers."

I grinned. I'd almost forgotten that story. "He was so nervous he only made it halfway up the ladder. And he was shaking so hard, he shook the paint can off the top."

Dad nodded. "The red paint spilled all on his head and down his neck. He rode his bicycle home so fast that the paint dried, coloring his hair and the back of his neck for good."

"I haven't thought of that story in such a long time."

"Your mother really wanted you to fit in and feel good about yourself. She thought from the start that you were special on the inside. I think that's why she knew you'd be okay when she had to go.

"See, you and me, we had each other to lean on. But your Mom, she blamed herself and she couldn't accept our help. All she felt was shame and guilt. I tried my best to keep her from leaving but she just couldn't hear it.

I know it hasn't been easy, Finny, but I think we've done okay."

There was so much I still didn't understand and maybe never would. Like why the one who lost the most was Abby. I mean, the rest of us had lives to live. All she got was remembered.

And why Mom turned her back on the chance to be part of our family. I used to think we were missing out, not having Mom around. But now I knew she was the one who really missed out. "You know what Dad?" I said. "We have done okay. We've done more than okay."

He took my hat off my head, just like the fortune-teller at the fair had done, then tousled my hair and put the hat back on a little crookeder than it had been before. "Finn Joseph, I think you're gonna be just fine."

The Big Race

Saturday morning graciously awakened us with cool, clear weather. It was finally race day. Do or die. Thank goodness. I told Piggyback that I'd be over around eleven to help him get ready. I begged him not to eat much before I got there. I could just see him barfing halfway down the track.

It was only eight-thirty, but I decided to call and remind him. He was as nervous as a long-tailed cat in a room full of rocking chairs. He looked at me with 'after school lunch' eyes and said, "You think it's too late to call the whole thing off? My stomach doesn't feel too good."

I gave him a glass of water and said, "It's just jitters. You'll settle down. Drink this, Champ."

We managed to get through the morning without incident and Piggyback seemed in good spirits. I had to call and double check with Pastor Davis. I had arranged for him to start the race because he had a starter's pistol and we wanted a neutral party to call the winner at the finish line just in case it was close at the finish. Probably wishful thinking on my part.

Everything was set, and it was time to get to the track. I did have a moment of doubt run through my mind before we left. Piggyback, Vinny and I were all little league all-stars in baseball. But to an awful lot of people we were real life second stringers. And that was kind of why we were going to the stadium today. I couldn't believe the people when we arrived at the stadium. I expected maybe fifty people but there were more than that in the first section of bleachers. It looked like mostly eighth graders in the first section and down closer to the announcers' booth in a small group of girls it was very difficult for me not to notice Veronica Marsh in her full-length coat and scarf like she was hosting the Macy's day parade.

Even Mr. Red was there, waving from the bleachers. One of the other kids must have told him about it. It struck me that he was one of us all along. People made fun of him all the time too. I bet he really caught grief when he was young. Mr. Red was an old school Different. Piggyback was in awe, with his mouth gaped open. "Hats, you gotta be kidding me. These people are here to watch us run? I can't do this."

I grabbed his shoulder and said, "They're here to watch you win. Now, get focused, man."

Piggyback slung his head toward the starting line and said, "Rock and roll, baby. Let's go."

He loped toward the track. We got to the start line and didn't see a Garrett anywhere. There were two distinct sections of onlookers in the stands, one at the start line and one at the finish. Piggyback began stretching out to prepare for the race and I stayed right with him. Two o'clock rolled around, and all our friends had made it. Pastor Davis was set up and ready and the Garretts still hadn't shown up. I asked the pastor to give them a little more time.

At about two-fifteen, out of a trail from the woods beyond the football field, all four of the Tracker boys appeared.

In true smart-aleck fashion, Herschel Garrett

walked onto the track in his cutoff overalls saying, "We wanted to give jug-butt a few extra minutes to get here, since his front end arrives ten minutes before his rear."

Piggyback and I were talking over some last second strategy, and from the enemy stands came a loud girl's voice, "You go get 'em, Piggyback! I know you can do it."

We looked at each other like, *did we both imagine that or what?* Because five rows up was Jeanine Rojas, otherwise known as Bulldog. And sitting right beside her was her little sister, Eugenia Grace, who, I have to say, looked pretty cool with the collar up on the coat that Claire had given her. For the first time, I realized I could see her as Grace.

As soon as we realized Grace had said it, Bulldog pushed her sister so hard that she fell two bleachers down. With a disdainful look at her sister, Grace got up, dusted herself off, and walked under the stands.

I spoke up since we were so late starting. "Are

we ready to race now?"

Everyone said yes. Pastor Davis had the runners take their marks, and he instructed them on his starting call.

I hit Piggyback in the arm, wished the big guy luck, and ran down to the other end of the track to the finish line to join Claire and Vinny. Claire gave me a wave from her power chair. Her crutches were strapped to the back, even though she wasn't supposed to be using them yet. Tommy had brought lawn chairs and was sitting just to the side of the track at the finish line.

When the gun sounded, I was locked in on the Kidd's every move. We had been through every scenario a million times, and I was trying to imagine what he was thinking.

Straight out of the gate, Piggyback slipped and went straight down hard. But did he panic? No, not our boy. This old sow plow ducked his head, rolled forward into a somersault and catapulted himself back into the race at full speed. He was five yards behind, but he had his opponents looking back. And with a determined, ferocious pace, George Hermann Kidd annihilated the ground before him, catching and passing Marshall Garrett.

Quickly, he built a head of steam, and after thirty yards or so, he was gaining speed, like an avalanching boulder, hurtling past Willard and Hermann like they were standing still.

Just as Piggyback pulled in front of Willard, Willard reached out and grabbed his shirt, pulling Piggyback backward and himself ahead again.

With a wordless bellow, the big guy lowered his head like a bull chasing red and cut to the outside lane, finding a gear he hadn't hit yet. He was now ahead of everyone except Herschel, and the sixty-yard mark was in their rear view. It was Herschel and Piggyback coming in like two freight trains merging on one track.

Herschel ran with his elbows out so every time Piggyback inched past him, Herschel could catch up and jab him in the ribs. It was back and forth like ping pong for a good way, and then they were both so tired coming down the stretch, it looked like anybody's race. Pastor Davis had strung a yellow tape across the finish line, and I decided to stand by one of the posts holding the tape as they came barreling in.

Everybody was going crazy, nervously cheering Piggyback on as this thing drew to a finish. Boy, was this gonna be a squeaker. They were shoulder to shoulder as the racers closed in to within five yards of the finish. In a great yawp, Piggyback let out this sound that I couldn't duplicate if I tried, and at the same time he thrust himself just past Herschel and dove over the finish line. The yellow tape snapped, the ends fluttering in the breeze. Like a giant balloon, Piggyback deflated and lay flat on his belly, arms stretched out wide, in the middle of the track.

He had done it. In drastic, dramatic, drop-dead Piggyback fashion, the Kidd had pulled it off. My fat, fabulous friend had just shamed the biggest bully in the whole town. Maybe the whole state.

Wow! It was like a movie. I was numb, but I had to make sure he wasn't dead. He hadn't moved from where he had collapsed.

Herschel Garrett, knowing he'd been beaten, hung his head straight to the ground and walked to the sideline of the football field. In a very methodical way, Herschel yanked the gold nugget necklace that he wore every single day, snapping it from his neck. In an explosive release of rage, he reached back like a quarterback and threw that necklace as hard as he could all the way across the football field, high into the opposite bleachers. You could hear the clanging of metal on metal echoing across the stadium.

Then he turned and walked away hard, like a mad six-year- old, toward the trail into the woods, kicking up grass every few yards, in anger.

Claire was out of her chair, leaning on a crutch, talking to Piggyback. "You were amazing, Georgie Porgie."

Piggyback was still laid out on his belly with his head cocked to one side, trying to talk in between gasps. "Thanks Claire," he said. "I think I sucked out every ounce of oxygen on this side of town. Little dizzy here. Whew! Is it hot in here or what?"

With my and Vinny's assistance, Piggyback managed to conjure the strength to slide over and sit up on the grass at the side of the track. Pastor Davis was nice enough to bring an ice chest full of bottled water for the guys running, plus anyone else who got thirsty. I grabbed one to bring over to Piggyback, and as I handed it to him, Grace walked up to congratulate him. He poured most of the water over his head. "You were awesome today, Piggyback. Congratulations."

Piggyback lifted his eyebrows and said, "Thanks so much, Grace. That means a lot. I saw you and your sister earlier. I'm sorry."

Grace looked down and said, "She thinks she's the boss of me, but she's not. I'm not like her. Anyway, I didn't come here to hang out with her. I came to watch you."

We all looked up as Claire's mom pulled up in their van, earlier than we'd expected. After a quick greeting, she opened the side door for Claire to drive her chair into the van and started to roll out the stadium gate. Claire, not to be silenced, hollered out the window, "Hats, are we still doing the bonfire tonight?"

"Heck yeah!" I pumped a fist in the air. "It's a celebration now. Six-thirty. My dad's making food. Don't be late." I turned to the champ and asked him quietly, "Why don't you ask your newest fan to the bonfire tonight? It's pretty obvious she likes you."

He was still catching his breath, but his eyes lit up. Between gasps, he said, "Think so? Guess I will." He staggered to his feet and before she could get away, he went up to Grace and said, "Hey, we're having a bonfire party tonight behind Hats' house if you wanna come? Six-thirty-ish."

She gave a quick nod and a grin that said it all. Then, eyes shining, Grace turned and walked away toward the other end of the track. With a parting glance over her shoulder at Piggyback she said, "See ya later, Stud."

Hats Off to Finn

The bonfire was great. Claire felt well enough to eat a cheeseburger, and Piggyback and Grace hit it off. None of the Garretts showed up to crash the party. The Differents were on a victory high all weekend. Then Monday rolled around.

Not a one of us was surprised back at school when Herschel balked at carrying Piggyback's books like he agreed upon losing the race. We knew he wasn't going to do it.

It didn't really matter anyway. Piggyback was getting a crazy amount of attention all over campus and I was as happy as a clam at high tide for him. Claire and I were talking at her locker, between classes. As I was telling her how proud I was of Piggyback, she thumped a crutch on the ground and slammed her locker door. I stopped in mid-sentence. What did she have to be annoyed about?

"You don't get it, do you?"

"Get what?"

Claire always had a way of cutting straight to the bone of what she was thinking. She looked me in the eye and said, "You know, Piggyback had very little to do with this whole transformation thing."

I cocked my head and looked at her like she was crazy. "Seriously? He just got through training his guts out and beating the pants off four jerks, way more athletic than he is."

Claire dropped her head, breathed in deep and let out one of those you're-so-stupid sighs. "Yeah. Now ask yourself why."

I looked at her blankly, and she blew out an exasperated breath. "Finn, have you stopped to think how much has happened to us in this one school year? And before you answer that, add to it what could have happened if *you* had handled things differently."

I couldn't help but grin at this girl. "How could I not think about it? Every time I lay my head down at night, I play another one out in my mind. And I wonder if we did right or not? If maybe I caused a lot of this trouble by creating the Differents."

Claire just kept looking at me sideways, like a puzzled Irish Setter. "You're still not seeing what we see. It was you who lifted all of us up. That wasn't a mistake."

I shrugged, with a tentative nod.

She smiled. "God's given you a gift to lift others. Somehow, you took a bunch of misfits and gave them a reason to believe in themselves. I'm proud of you, Finn McCleary."

I really didn't know how to respond to this, but she was gut shooting me pretty hard. "Claire, I was just sick and tired of being a door mat and seeing my friends get picked on. We changed all that, didn't we? Or at least put a dent in it?"

She grinned, a grin as big as her heart. "We sure did, Finn McCleary. We surely did."

Remember My Name

We were peacefully sitting on Claire's porch and from the fence came a thundering crash. She had asked me to come over after school because we hadn't, in her opinion, finished our discussion from earlier. Girls, I swear. If talking was an Olympic event, they'd have more medals than they do shoes. I hadn't been there ten minutes and the storm hit. Vinny and Piggyback popped their heads over the gate, like two weird-looking jack-in-the-boxes.

"Is this a private party?" Piggyback yelled out across the yard. "Sorry Claire, I kind of wrecked my bike into your fence. Vinny cut me off."

Vinny pushed him in the arm and said, "He's been using the Flintstone braking system ever since I've known him! Your dad told us where you were, Hats. We needed to talk to you and Claire both."

Claire waved them both into the yard and said, "Come onto the porch, guys. I'm going to get some more tea. Be right back."

I looked at both of them like they were crazy and asked them what was so important.

"Well," Vinny said. "Herschel just won't let it go, man. He chased me and Piggyback for three blocks coming over here. The whole time he was yelling about you, Hats. Apparently, now he thinks you tricked him into the race with Piggyback."

Piggyback started to laugh. "I guess we're leaving out details like I outran that crybaby, huh?"

Vinny nodded and high-fived Piggyback. "Problem is," Vinny said, "he's probably headed this way right now."

Everybody was getting worked up over nothing, so I said, "Guys, take it easy, will ya, please? I'm not getting my nerves in a tizzy over Herschel Garrett ever again. Let him come. What's he gonna do?"

Claire came out balancing the tea pitcher pinned between her hip and the inside of one crutch. She eased it down, then leaned over to my ear and asked, "Are you worried about Herschel showing up here?"

I looked into her eyes and said, "I can handle it. Don't worry, k?"

Piggyback was out of his chair again and talking fast. "He's coming, guys. I can hear that crappy motorcycle he made in metal-shop coming this way. Hats, get out of here, man. He's coming for you. Maybe we should call the cops?"

The words were barely out of his mouth when Herschel drove his motorcycle up beside Claire's fence and revved up his puny little engine. A couple of minutes later, Marshall, Willard and Hermann rode up from behind on their bikes, huffing and puffing from exhaustion.

Vinny turned to me and said, "We got this, right, Hats?"

"You know me, Vin. I don't like countin' my peaches 'fore they're fuzzed up good, but this one is in the bag. You guys stay behind me, okay?"

I drank down the rest of my tea like I was

Humphrey Bogart and it was scotch whiskey. I sat the glass down hard on the table and glared out at Garrett, who was just sitting there. I yelled out to him, "You lost? This is private property, you know."

He just sat there and stared. I guess I was supposed to be intimidated or something. Whatever.

Mrs. Hanover came out and asked me if there was a problem she needed to handle. I kept my eyes on Hershel and said, "No, ma'am. I'm going to give this guy some GPS pointers. I think he lost his way."

"But Finn—" Claire said.

"Claire," I said, "please stop worrying. We've already beaten him. You can see it in his eyes. All he can do is threaten. That's really all he could ever do."

Claire seared me with cat eyes and stomped her crutch hard on the porch. "I'm part of this, Finn McCleary." She walked close behind me, readied for battle.

I walked out to the fence and through the gate with my friends following close behind. I paused to look at them, Claire with her eyes blazing, Vinny with his fists clenched, Piggyback with his jaw tight and his chest stuck out, all of them ready to rush into the breach with me. Claire might be right that I had made them strong, but they made me strong too.

I thought of the fortune teller, how she told me about low places in the road. Before now, I thought that was the only road I'd ever travel. With the help of these friends, we not only saw this situation more clearly by choosing to change our course, but we were changing our future, once and for all. She'd even been right about Claire's words changing lives, because they'd sure changed mine. Now it was time to listen to the rest of the old woman's message and measure what I was made of.

I stretched my hand behind me toward my friends, palm out in a *stop* signal, and stepped forward. I wanted to get Herschel and I separated a bit.

Finally, Herschel said, "You think you're smart, don't you?"

I had this thought before I answered. Piggyback had asked me once if I thought God looked out for people, and I remembered telling him that I thought He had to. I must have felt like I needed a little looking out for in that moment, to have thought of that.

"Yes, Hershey," I said to Herschel. "It's the one thing I have going for me, actually. And I'm gonna tell you something, here and now. You don't have to like me or any of my friends, but we're done being called names and being treated like before. You don't scare me anymore."

Herschel scowled and said, "I could break you in half, little boy."

I was feeling fearless like never before. I think I knew how Columbus felt, finding another world.

I said, "Think again, Herschel. You could break me in half, but you won't. You know why? Cause you're a barker, not a biter."

He sucked in a sharp breath. "You're gonna think bite, Freak," he mumbled, and looked around as if to make sure his cronies were backing him.

I laughed. "We've embarrassed you more than once and I don't really like doing it, but it's not that hard to do. So, unless you want more of it, remember my name. It should be easy. You're good with four letter words. Now, pay attention. F-I-N-N, Finn. That's my name. Now get the heck out of our neighborhood. Don't you have a temper tantrum to pick up at the stadium?"

Piggyback stepped up from behind me, digging into his pant pocket. "Hang on, Finn. It's in here somewhere. Dang it! It's stuck on my britches." Piggyback yanked and yanked on the pocket of his pants, and finally he pulled out Herschel's gold necklace. He twirled it around his index finger. "Is this the tantrum you're talking about? It'd make a good collar for Gus, don't you think? Yeah, it was just lying there shinin' in the dirt. Right under the stands, Herschel. The clasp wasn't even broken. I just bent it back into place. Good arm, by the way."

I shot Piggyback a glare and said, "Can you give it to me, please?"

He handed it over, and I held it close to my mouth and blew the gob of pocket lint off it.

I took another step closer toward Herschel Garrett. His minions were standing on the side of the road chewing on long reeds of grass, like Jersey cows. I ignored them and said to Herschel, "We've never been friends, but I've known you ever since we were little kids. And I know for a fact that you've been wearing this necklace for a long time. So here, take it. You don't have to take it in friendship. But do we really have to hate each other anymore?"

I held it out and it spun in the light. I felt a pang, thinking of how his mom must have loved him, and how much he must miss her. That was one thing we had in common. Only his mom was never coming back, and there was still a chance mine might.

Herschel grabbed the necklace and spun his motorcycle around and peeled out of the neighborhood. I stood with my arms folded as the rocks and dust flew past my feet and then I ran a few yards in his trail. I couldn't help sounding off one last triumphant bullet. "Hey Garrett! Just try to remember, will ya? The name's Finn. Finn McCleary."

Herschel sped out of there, that necklace dangling from his handlebar. He pulled a wheelie, turning his head back. With his black hair blowing in his face, he yelled to me, "Catch ya later, Finn McCleary!"

9 781952 754821